Felicity Flipflops

Felicity Flipflops

Dawn M. Gelston

ISBN, paperback: 978-1-80227-364-9
ISBN, ebook: 978-1-80227-365-6

This book is typeset in Garamond Premier Pro

*For the late Leo Flanagan, the teacher who
nurtured and encouraged my love for writing
and had the most impact on me.*

CONTENTS

ACKNOWLEDGEMENTS

To all the people I love.

To all the people who have listened to me and reassured me when I've been doubtful of my abilities.

To the children I currently teach, thank you for inspiring me and encouraging me daily. You brighten up each day for me.

To my parents who have always supported and guided me in every endeavour.

To my sisters Shona, Aisling and Janine, plus my cousins, aunts and uncles, who always want the best for me.

To my friend Leanne, who has been there every step of the way with her words of wisdom and constant support.

To my friend Brendan, who has always been my biggest believer, I can't thank you enough for everything.

To my nephews Shea and Brendan and nieces Cara, Caoimhe, Ava and Isla, I love you all more than you know.

To all my friends - you know who you are. Thank you for your encouragement.

To my brother Paul, the person who is my confidante and has always helped me believe in myself, I thank you a million times over.

To my publishing company, Publishing Push, thank you for your support and guidance the whole way through.

To my amazing illustrator, thank you for your patience.

To the readers, I hope you enjoy the story of Felicity and her friends and learn that it's okay to be you; it's okay to be who you want to be.

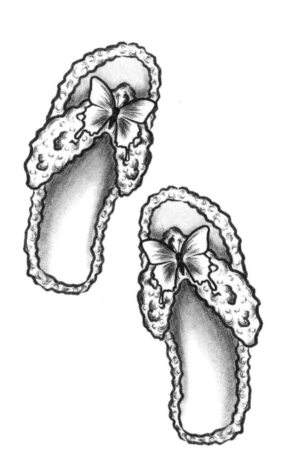

CHAPTER 1

MISS 'MINDFULNESS' GREEN

Miss Green's classroom wasn't your typical classroom. Well, in comparison to what adults, especially grandparents, tell us about their time at school.

Adult quote example 1:

"In my day, you sat at a single table facing the front of the classroom, and you daren't have spoken unless you were asked a question. You answered straight away, too – what is with this 'thinking time' you tell me about?"

Miss Green allowed all children to talk to each other (most of the time, that is). In fact, in her eyes, if you weren't conversing in groups or pairs, you weren't learning.

Adult quote example 2:

"School was purely academic, usually made up of hours of constant, tedious, rote-learning. Health and Wellbeing? Mindfulness? There was no such thing in our day. The only thing we'd to be mindful of was not to breathe too loudly or sit the wrong way, for fear of a blackboard duster landing on your head and knocking you out..."

I couldn't believe it when my grandma told me this was a regular occurrence in her classroom. I was bewildered... how did teachers actually get away with this type of violence? My favourite person in the whole of the world didn't tend to tell fibs, but surely this wasn't true...

The Year Six teacher at St. Bernadette's Primary School, Miss Green, was all about teaching children *skills for life*. She wanted to prepare us, academically and emotionally, for the world of work and the "*tricky challenges* of life," as she called them.

"Not in a negative way, but in a realistic way," she would tell us.

In her class, you talked about feelings and what it's like to be human, not just a law-abiding, one-hundred-percent-attention-giving student. Or a robot.

Most children came out of her lessons at the end of the day with a spring in their step, while the rest of the school patiently awaited their turn to be taught by her: a caring and unconventional class teacher.

Maybe the fact that her room was a 'soothing room' (as she liked to call it) had something to do with it, too. It had a corner area adorned with comfy cushions, a tepee tent and calming blue beanbags. I mean, isn't it any child's dream? A break from lessons and a place to lie in the clouds in a candyfloss haven and forget you're in school for a while?

Miss Green's popularity was much to the repugnance of the hateful, hunchbacked headteacher, Ms Bowman, who, as well as her camelback, had the thinnest, longest legs known to man and coarse, wispy hairs dangling from her chiselled chin (you will soon fully understand the extent of the ghastly sight of this hideous, humpy human).

I will never forget the first time I witnessed the raging rants of that hag of a woman. One afternoon, during my first week at the school, she appeared at the doorway, her beady eyes glaring through her steel-rimmed glasses, and summoned Miss Green out of the classroom and into the corridor for a scolding.

"I've been looking at your daily timetable."

"You have?" asked Miss Green.

"Yes, I have!" she frowned, disgusted that the Board of Governors had employed someone who didn't bow down to her every word.

"I do not think," she continued, "in fact I know, there is NO need for these mindfulness and movement break *thingy-ma-bobby* sessions, or whatever you call them! Not every day of the week!"

Slimy spit splashed onto Miss Green's right eyebrow, and she took a step back, wiping the salty splurge off with her sleeve. The teacher, a tall, blonde, thirty-something-year-old with oval-shaped glasses and an extensive collection of animal earrings, cleared her throat.

"Ms Bowman, we've been through this. There is EVERY need!"

Fixing the right leg of her glasses onto her ears, she added, "It has been discussed and agreed at our recent staff day, you know, the one you missed when you were ill.." she taunted her. "All teachers, including the Deputy Head, of course, agreed that, when we have sufficiently covered the curriculum, we have the autonomy to choose which activities we feel are beneficial to our class last period of the day. Did Mr Flatley not tell you?" she smirked.

Ms Bowman's wrinkly, triangular-shaped neck was covered in blood-red blotches, and steam practically belched from her ears.

"Mr Flatley? No! No, he did not!" she roared. A rumble of rage made its way up the hallway.

"You see, Ms Bowman," said Miss Green, confidently, "children nowadays are forced to live in a world filled with worries, a world where looks and appearance are considered as indicators of worth in a person..."

"Okay!!" hissed Ms Bowman, her bony left hand perched on her hip, the other curled around her walking stick. "I don't need one of your worldly lectures..."

"Excuse me?" gasped Miss Green.

The hideous headmistress spun away from the teacher and scurried up the corridor as fast as the metre sticks and her wonky walking aid could carry her, spitting and leaving a saliva trail behind her.

"Teachers doing as they please in MY school will not be happening!"

"Oh, it's already in the new school handbook!" Miss Green yelled after her.

SLAM went the office door. Even its poor hinges screeched for help.

Miss Green chuckled to herself, and feeling like she'd just won a 200-metre sprint, she pushed in the back of one of her ginger cat earrings and re-entered the classroom. The whole class, panicking, tried to give the impression they'd been uninterested in the conversation outside. They had, in fact, stopped dead to earwig when their teacher had left the room, of course, and had listened to every word exchanged in the corridor.

"Children," said Miss Green loudly, standing in the middle of the classroom.

Twenty-seven heads instantly turned to direct their attention, gazing up at her like she was some sort of goddess or celebrity.

"Another thing we must remember. Never EVER be afraid to challenge someone when you disagree with them. Of course, there are appropriate ways to do this. But don't EVER let someone talk you down. If you believe in something, voice it...have your say!"

She did like the word *ever*, I noticed.

"We will!" shouted Billy Barlow. "You were very brave there, Miss... I... I mean, you *told* her!! Ms Bowman was told!" he sniggered.

Miss Green turned her head away and walked towards the whiteboard to hide her giggles at Billy's praise.

"I'm afraid I can't comment too much on that, Billy, but all I will say is, I like to stand my ground. My mother taught me how to do that," she smiled reminiscently.

The 6A class was filled with many interesting and troublesome characters. Not troublesome in a bad sense of the word, just a group of children who'd been through unfortunate times of late and could sometimes be a *little* draining on the only adult in the room. Well, most times.

Billy, a small, slightly-pudgy, old-before-his-time, likeable lad, and the one who had just complimented Miss Green's assertive actions, had cried most days since the beginning of term. His parents had divorced during the summer holidays, and he was completely and utterly devastated. He was recently beginning to manage his emotions a little better, though, and was only bursting into loud sobs about once or twice a day now, instead of his previous daily average of around seventeen times. Poor Billy.

Miss Green had continuously commended and comforted him through his cascading tears. She told him he was a courageous young man, being able to express his emotions and paving the way for other young men to do the same without worrying about how it looked to others. Without thinking it made them look feeble, too. It did quite the opposite in her eyes; it showed great strength.

"And why should boys or men not cry when they need to? Why should they sit, straining to keep their emotions inside?" she asked the class the last time Billy had started to wail uncontrollably. "It's about time there was no person, regardless of gender, who should think they must keep in all their feelings and be afraid to tell someone or show them how they're *actually* feeling. We are all only human, and life is tough, tough to say the least!! It's a false, social-media-obsessed planet we're living on. We need to be able to ask for help when we need it! We need to show our emotions, let it all out! Banish the shame of sharing *real* feelings!"

Our very passionate teacher was adamant that our class would lead the way and make a difference to others. She wanted 'mental health and wellbeing' lessons to be compulsory on the school curriculum, not just in County Mayo but throughout Ireland, as far as she could possibly make it happen.

Second on the list, in no particular order (of need or distress), was Jenny Jackson. Jenny was morbidly and dangerously obese. She always wore her hair in pigtails with unmatching ribbons and looked a bit like an oversized toddler. Though always jovial, Jenny was an emotional overeater. Ever since she lost her "Pops" (beloved grandad) to cancer about two years ago, she had been using food to help her cope – to help her get through her days without his humour and happy face.

Despite Miss Green's earnest efforts to counsel and advise her, Jenny was still consuming, between humongous, fat-riddled meals, around three Cadbury's Flakes and six packets of Tayto Cheese and Onion crisps a day. And that was just at school. Miss Green's carpenter brother made Jenny a sturdy, more comfortable seat for the classroom, as the chairs made only to hold the weight of the average 11-year-old child had groaned every time she sat on them. Miss Green and Jenny herself knew she was massively overweight, but the plastic chairs didn't need to continuously bring it to the attention of others, creaking and squeaking about the place all day long.

Sienna Sorski was another child with a few troubles, to say the least. A filthy-rich heir to Sorski Jewellery (a spin-off of Swarovski), an 'at times' socially-awkward Sienna spent every day with her nanny, Lydia, a retired jockey from Switzerland. Meanwhile, her parents were constantly flying in their private jet to different destinations across the world, flogging and supplying diamond necklaces and rings to jewellery companies and rich Western families. She had her own swimming pool, pony, stables, farm and dance studio, but as clichéd as it sounds, all Sienna ever really longed for was a sibling to share her wealthy lifestyle with. And parents who could be around, even just for half of the year, would also be nice. Was this too much to ask?

Lydia, the nanny, although she tried her best, was not programmed or equipped to deal with Sienna and her tiresome tantrums and long-winded *huffathons* (huffing and being stubborn when one doesn't get their own way for a considerable amount of hours, sometimes days).

She was often left distressed, calling Miss Green for advice when Sienna was 'off on one.' The class teacher had advised Lydia to ensure there were consequences for Sienna's actions. Even losing a ride on the pony, a swim in the pool or dance lesson, she said, would help stroppy Sienna learn the difference between 'right and wrong behaviour choices.'

The exhausted nanny had tried to follow through on banning a pony lesson last week, but Sienna had screamed, banged and slammed doors for two and a half hours straight causing Lydia to develop the worst migraine imaginable. To allow herself to recover in a darkened room, she backed down and off Sienna hopped and popped to ride her precious pony, who also happened to be named *Precious*.

Then there was me... Felicity Flanagan: the girl who happens to be telling this story. The story which, when you reach the end, I hope makes you feel a sense of gratitude for what you have in your life. You may even take away a tiny bit of advice from our remarkable class teacher when it comes to talking about your feelings and not being afraid to. Enough of all that for now, though... a *little* more about me.

Well, you probably wouldn't believe it, but up until quite recently, I wasn't really able to tell anyone *anything* about me. Not. One. Single. Thing.

In fact, I had always found it really hard to open my mouth and talk to other human beings in general. Even one-word replies were a challenge for me. The words would simply fail to come out. Until a few months ago, I could hardly even give people eye contact. I was the most awkward child. EVER.

When Miss Green was talking about kids having it 'tough,' I suppose she had another one added to her list the day I arrived at St. Bernadette's.

I don't live with my real family. Or in what some people think of as a *typical* family either.

Instead, I live with my foster mum, Bella Beaumont. Just Bella, a seamstress, her sewing room of a squillion fabrics and me, in her cosy, detached house beside the beach in the small, close-knit town of Alcora, County Mayo, in the West of Ireland.

Surprisingly, I had liked my new school straight away (aside from Ms Bowman, of course). Full of the wackiest, most oddly likeable combination of people you'd ever wish to be introduced to, it really felt like one of the best places to go to school on the Emerald Isle (if you agree that going to school isn't the worst thing in the world, that is). I didn't feel completely grateful about the place at the beginning, however.

For a timid, awkward girl like me, even the thought of starting another new school was a daunting, gut-wrenchingly nervous experience. The description of St. Bernadette's from Bella as being *a middle-sized school, slightly older-looking than some, not far from the Catholic Church,* didn't paint an appealing picture in my mind. I was pleasantly surprised to find out the school wasn't as outdated as it looked on the outside. Its plaque read, 'Built in 1857,' and the building genuinely looked like it hadn't been refurbished since the Victorian era, with its drab, grey stone walls and rusted bell tower.

Inside, I was pleased to discover there actually was an internet connection and semi-up-to-date facilities like an IT suite, iPads in some classrooms and a large sports hall.

The fateful morning quickly arrived, and being greeted at the doorway by the headmistress, Bog Breath Bowman, as she had rightfully been nicknamed, did not help my somersaulting stomach. Bella had been up most of the night strumming on her sewing machine. She was even more nervous than me and looked like she hadn't slept a single second, swigging her third coffee as fast as she could and failing to pretend she wasn't absolutely exhausted before we left the house.

"Listen, my darling; you will be fine," she reassured me as we slowly trudged side-by-side up the uneven, concrete-slabbed steps of the crumbling building.

What was ahead of me?

"I told you I went to this school, didn't I? And you know, your teacher, Miss Green, I actually went to school with her!"

"Yes, you've already told me about twenty times!" I snapped at her, rolling my eyes towards the sky. Instantly regretting my sharp reply, I tried to take it back by giving her a weary, poor effort of a smile.

I was more comfortable with Bella than I'd been with any of my other foster mums, but sometimes my emotions would get the better of me, and I'd grunt at her. I was never proud of this, but I think she knew I never really meant it. She had actually understood me really well from the beginning, and that wasn't an easy task; I knew that much.

Back to the first day...

I could smell Bowman's stale, nauseating breath from about eight feet away as she awkwardly approached us. My chin dropped and almost hit off my collar bone at the sight of the metre-stick-thin legs she owned. They looked like they'd snap into smithereens any second. I wondered how the sticks, covered in thick, spiky hairs like bristles on a yard brush, carried the weight of her tall, over-arched body. The sudden appearance of long, crooked fingers like tree branches reaching out to shake my hand made me shudder. Reluctantly, I shook the scrawny hand for about a nanosecond.

She grinned at me. Waves of stinky breath escaped through the gaps at the side of her mouth as she smiled down at me, revealing a spear-headed, dangly tongue and teeth like tiny, grey gravestones. My eyes literally hung out of the sockets at the sight of her.

"Welcome to St. Bernadette's Primary School," said Ms Bowman, in a husky, manly voice.

There was nothing redeeming about this woman in the slightest.

Bella, clearly trying to hide her retches from the pong of the breath, stepped subtly to the side away from her as we walked up the corridor.

"Thank you, Ms Bowman," she replied, with a fake smile plastered across her face, like the one she did when the social worker visited us.

"It's been a while since I've been here," she continued, grinning through gritted teeth.

"Indeed! I do remember you, Ms Beaumont. Very arty, I recall. And now look at you," she ground her headstones. "Taking in lovely children and being so very, very kind."

Did she just say *taking in?*

"Well, it's actually thanks to the values instilled by the headteacher when I was in my first few years of school here, Mrs Finnegan. Wonderful lady. She left her mark, that's for sure! She taught us all to be kind and give to others. In fact, the locals in the town would still say how she was the best teacher we ever had in the history of the school."

Good on you, Bella, I thought, tempted to high-five her for putting the awful woman in her place.

"Is that right? The locals would say that, would they?" scowled Ms Bowman, with disgust written all over her shrivelled face. Her eyes widened behind her unflattering, outdated glasses that hung down from the sides of her ears in a silver chain.

"Please, come in and sit down, both of you," she said, as we entered her office. She pointed at two cold-looking leather chairs on the opposite side of her desk.

Tattered and torn, just like its owner, the office chair let out a wail for help as she sat her bottom onto it. Even it hated her.

"I think that needs a bit of WD-40 rubbed on it," said Bella, looking at the long-past-its-time seat.

I had no idea what that WD-thing was.

"Hmm, well, that's a job for the caretaker, not me!" hissed Bowman.

A few painful minutes later, after a very bored Bella and I had convincingly pretended to listen to the riveting rules and routines of the school, Bella was reluctantly clambering down the steps towards the car. She hugged me like she was never going to see me again and looked back with tear-filled eyes as she waved her goodbyes.

I told you she was hideous, didn't I?

I was left alone with Bog Breath. Petrified, I glared at the statues of, who I now know as Our Lady and Jesus, on my commentated tour of the school and the seemingly never-ending journey to my new classroom.

As we walked up the corridor, we were met by a tall, dark-haired man wearing a collar.

"This is Father Brennan," said Bowman, grinning widely all of a sudden. He took a step back away from her face (the breath, no doubt).

"Very pleased to meet you," he smiled, lifting my right hand and shaking it firmly, without giving me a choice.

"Father Brennan is a regular visitor to our school, Felicity. He celebrates mass every Monday morning for all the children."

I managed an awkward smile, briefly looking up at him from the dusty, grey, definitely-Victorian tiles.

"I'll be seeing you soon, Ph... Ph... Phoebe," he said, as he walked off in the direction of the canteen, "and good luck for your first day. Ms Bowman will be good to you, don't worry," he said reassuringly.

I'm not so sure, I thought.

Bog Breath lurked behind me outside the 6A classroom. My new teacher, who, thanks to Bella, I was well aware went by the name of Miss Green, came out to the corridor to greet me. She smiled warmly.

"Thanks, Ms Bowman. I'll just have a quick chat with Felicity first before we go in."

My newest class teacher wore a flowy, green dress and dolphin earrings. She had very kind, genuine eyes. Not that teachers couldn't have kind eyes, but there was something quite normal about her. I had the feeling she wasn't going to be a power-tripping teacher like some of my old ones. These types of teachers love to be in control of people younger than them and seem to get gratification out of embarrassing them and getting them to do as they say, straight away. There was nothing threatening at all about Miss Green; she seemed far from this type, and I really hoped my first impressions of her were right.

Bog Breath, taking the hint, wished me a good day and flew like a whirlwind up the hallway, even with the walking stick. As she went, she roared at a young, terrified child to stop running.

"I can't tell you how excited we've all been to meet you, Felicity," said the newly-acquainted Miss Green.

I felt like running out the front door of the building and could barely look at

her.

"One thing I want you to know is, you will be fine in this class. We all work together and support one another. You won't be on your own. The other children are great and really friendly."

That will be a first, I thought.

"Okay," I mumbled awkwardly.

"Oh, I do like your shoes," she grinned.

I hesitated. "They're more of a flipflop."

"Well, they are very nice. Different, I like different…"

That *was* actually a first, I thought.

A minute later, I was in the classroom seated beside Edna Evans, a girl who looked a little bit like a boy. Her hair was cropped short, and she seemed completely disinterested in what was going on around her. I was so relieved to find that my entrance went without any fuss. The children were occupied competing against each other on some iPad maths game and didn't seem to flinch at my arrival.

"Edna's the name. I know you'd think it was Edward," she tittered.

"Hi. Felicity is mine," I managed to mutter back to her.

"It's a bit…em…busy in here," she smiled. "Don't worry, though; you'll be okay here. Best and craziest class in the school."

"Thanks," I said shyly.

"Those look nice and warm," she said awkwardly, nodding towards my flipflops.

"Yeah, they are," I replied, slightly embarrassed.

"Cool, though, I like them," she replied. "They look pretty cool."

I wasn't sure if she was pretending, but I didn't care. Already, I knew I was going to like this girl.

A few hours later, after individual introductions to my new classmates had taken place, I was beginning to feel quite relaxed. I was slightly scared by some of my peers in the rowdy room, but not feeling as out of place as I thought I was going to.

I had missed quite a bit of school to date, but I was enjoying the experience and mixture of personalities around me. Edna, Miss Green informed me, was my 'learning partner'. Basically, this meant I worked with her in most subjects, and if I understood something, I shared it with her and vice versa. I didn't have much knowledge to share of anything really and still felt a little embarrassed, but it definitely didn't feel like my old school – the one that hadn't moved on much from my grandma's era. I'd point-blank refused to go to this school; I was yelled at when I didn't know what 34 x 20 was in precisely three seconds. I felt less self-conscious here already. Edna and I could work out the answers together (or try to) and make mistakes together. It really didn't matter in this place, in Miss Green's classroom, anyway.

My first 'mindfulness meditation' session was one of the strangest experiences ever. Well, the weirdest thing I'd been a part of at school, until then.

We were sprawled on top of soft bean bags on the floor listening to the singer, Enya. I struggled to hide my yawns. Bella would usually listen to her music when she had a dressmaking deadline to help her de-stress, so I knew exactly who she was. Her soothing voice would send anyone off to the land of nod. For hours. For days. For eternity.

After at least six attempts, I eventually settled into the breathing exercises. I tittered at the beginning, but it was very obvious that class 6A took the sessions seriously; they had their desks tidied in seconds and were plonked on the floor before Miss Green had finished saying, *"It's time for mindfulness."*

After a few seconds of the activity, I opened my eyes and sneakily scanned the room, trying not to let the teacher catch me. She sat on a mat at the front of the classroom with her knees tucked underneath her bottom (I later learnt this was the thunderbolt yoga pose). Billy Barlow had slimy drool dangling from his jaw and was completely out of it. Jenny Jackson let out a loud snort, and the whole class burst into hysteria.

"Eh! I was drifting off into a nice dream there," spluttered Jenny, stretching out her arms.

"Children, back to calm at once, please!" exclaimed Miss Green. She threw looks of disappointment around the room and then focused her attention back on Jenny.

"Jenny, as I've said several times before, we must not use these sessions as a time to sleep. A time to relax, yes, of course, but not sleep. Remember our health plan," she smiled at her encouragingly.

"Yes, Miss," Jenny replied. "I did go to bed at about 11 o'clock last night."

"Well, that's an improvement. Too late still, but a marked improvement!"

Sienna Sorski was clearly not enjoying it as much as the rest of us.

She was groaning aloud and wriggling around on the floor. Her shiny, black hair was tied up in a ponytail, and she was impeccably dressed in perfect white ankle socks and shimmering black shoes. She had set her *expensive* Louis Vuitton school bag that she had bragged about earlier beside her, despite being told to place it under the table at the beginning of the activity.

"My back is so sore!" she winced.

"Sienna! What have we said about shouting out in class?" asked our teacher in what seemed a louder-than-usual voice. "There *will be* consequences if this continues! And put that bag under your desk immediately! That's twice now I've had to give you that instruction!"

This was the first time I'd witnessed Miss Green seem genuinely cross.

"Sorry, Miss," she said, struggling to get up and lift her lavish bag, "I was riding Precious yesterday for hours, and my back is really sore."

"I see. Maybe a swim in your pool this evening will help your back," replied Miss Green, looking a little less annoyed than she was a few seconds earlier.

"Hmm, maybe. I don't like the pool, though; it's got too much chlorine in it at the minute and wrecks my hair."

"Oh dear," butted in Martha Molloy, "that's absolutely terrible! Does your maid not brush the stinky chlorine out for you?" she asked her.

Martha had brown, bobbed hair and chestnut brown eyes. She looked much older than ten or eleven.

"I don't have a maid!" snapped Sienna back at her. "I have a nanny!"

"Oh, pardon me," answered Martha. "It's the same thing, is it not?!"

"It is not!" replied Sienna abruptly.

"Sienna and Martha, that is enough!" said the teacher firmly.

I could sense from the gasps around the room that Miss Green raising her voice twice in a short space of time wasn't something that happened too often.

"Now! Let's all get back to the breathing... Close your eyes again, everyone," she continued, in a lower, more gentle voice, "and as you inhale and exhale, I want you to imagine a happy, tranquil place. Think about where you'd most like to be in the whole world right now – perhaps not even in this world, maybe another world... a place where you'd go to feel happy and content. Imagine you are there now, or heading there, at this very moment..."

I pushed my feet further into my flipflops. The fluffy lining Bella had made for the autumn season felt so warm and toasty. I was immediately in my happy place. They *were* my happy place.

"Where are you, Jeffrey?" Miss Green inquired.

Jeffrey, a quiet, tall, dangly-looking boy, replied, "Well... I'm part of a space mission, just about to step out onto Mars for the first time."

He smiled widely, seeming chuffed with his effort.

"Mars?" asked Miss Green. "How wonderful that would be, Jeffrey! We'd need a little more oxygen there first, wouldn't we?" she asked the room of mellow children. The audience nodded up at her.

"Now, Martha, what about you? Where are you?" she asked.

"I'm lying in a hammock in Spain, swaying in the warm breeze. I'm licking one of my five scoops of mint chocolate chip ice cream," she answered, giggling.

"Great description and sounds delightful. I'd go for vanilla myself and maybe just the two scoops," replied Miss Green, with a happier grin.

"Remember, children, if you don't wish to share, you don't have to," she added.

Phew, I breathed. I was definitely not going to speak out in class. Not. A. Chance.

Dawn M. Gelston

CHAPTER 2

LUMPY, CLUMPY, CURDLED CUSTARD

My first lunchtime experience happened to fall on *Tuesday Treat Day* (I later learnt this meant dessert was served on the second school day of the week and on no other day). St. Bernadette's was a healthy-eating school, apparently.

Remembering what day it was, just before the bell went for lunch, Jenny almost burst a lung jumping around the classroom with excitement. I could tell she tested Miss Green's patience as she would subtly take deep breaths in the build-up to speaking to the excitable 11-year-old.

"I can see you're thrilled for Tuesday Treat Day, Jenny," said the patient teacher, "but we must stand still, line up quietly and enter the dining room nice and calmly."

"I will," said Jenny, literally licking her lips as she stomped towards the top of the line.

The other children in the class didn't look as amused, I noticed.

"I'm guessing the treat's good?" I whispered to Edna behind me in the line.

'It'll be like warm, salty vomit served in a bowl," she replied.

"Can't wait," I mouthed back at her, smiling. At least she had prepared me for the culinary treat ahead.

Inside the dining room, children lined up like military soldiers and immediately sat when commanded to by Bog Breath. We were perched on long benches, about twenty of us crammed together on a hard, backless seat. Father Brennan was there, and Bowman spoke to us all with a lower tone of voice. Still croaky, but softer.

"Children, we have the pleasure of Father Brennan's presence today," she grinned from the top of the hall, displaying those grey, gritted gnashers. "His Reverend Father will say Grace before meals," she continued.

"Who's Grace?" I quietly asked Edna, who was sitting beside me, sighing with boredom. It was the first time I'd noticed she was wearing trousers.

"Grace isn't a person," she giggled quietly.

I felt my throat warm up.

"Don't worry, it's one of the twenty-five prayers you'll get to know," she reassured me.

Father Brennan stood at the front of the brightly-painted gymnasium, surrounded by walls clad with 'wonderful work' examples, all eyes on him. His hands were joined, and he began to say the unfamiliar prayer. The only words I could really make out from it were *Bless us.* Realising I was the only one not speaking along with him, I awkwardly began to mime, trying to keep in time with the other children. Thankfully, it was very short, so I didn't have to bluff that I knew the 'prayer before meals' for that long.

A few minutes later, we were presented with a plate of squidgy, soggy fish and chips, dunked in a river of grease. The nasty smell made me feel a bit queasy. After covering the contents with about twelve dollops of ketchup and an extremely generous helping of vinegar, I managed to eat about five chips. The fish could stay where it was. Jenny, who sat opposite us, had devoured her meal in less than seventeen seconds.

Sienna refused to eat as much as a bite of a chip and sat across the table from me, sulking like a spoilt toddler with her arms folded.

"I'm going to be sick at the smell of that... that muck," she scowled, pushing the plate away from her.

"Something wrong with the food?" interrupted a tiny lady, who appeared out of nowhere. She was wearing a navy trouser-suit and red lipstick, which was smudged around her lips.

"Emm, no... no... Mrs Rodgers," stammered a very startled Sienna, fidgeting in her seat.

"Good, because there are many people in God's kingdom who would be delighted *AND* beyond grateful for the meal you have right there in front of you!"

"I know," answered Sienna, trying to look enthused and pulling the plate back towards her. The woman turned on her heels and clip-clopped over to the other side of the room.

"That's Religious Rodgers," Edna informed me. "Constantly talks about God, his work and his kingdom and sneaks up on you when you least expect it."

"I figured that," I replied with a chuckle.

Sienna suddenly flung her fish onto Jenny's plate.

"Please eat it for me, Jenny! Please!" she begged.

Without much convincing or pleading required, Jenny clasped the fish in her bare right hand and bit into it like a grizzly bear biting into a freshly-caught piece of salmon. The crumbly haddock had made the quick journey down her oesophagus before you could say the words, *Tuesday Treat*.

All of a sudden, a loud clip-clapping, tap-tapping sound came from the middle of the dining room. Alarmed, I jumped back, almost falling off the bench.

My mouth automatically dropped open at the sight in front of me. A man wearing leather shoes with a heel, tight trousers and a sparkling, sequined shirt was flinging his legs in the air, vigorously tapping down on the hard, wooden dining room floor at around twenty miles per hour. This man almost looked berserk; he was that fast on his feet. His greying hair was tied back, and he proudly kept his hands on his hips as he went.

Why was I the only one alarmed at this? I was baffled.

CLICK.CLICK.CLICK. Then CLACK! It came to a sharp, dramatic halt. The man now stood with his arms raised like a peacock's feathers, his right leg and toes pointing to the floor.

"St. Bernadette's pupils!!" exclaimed this frantic, leg-flying human. "You can now go, table by table, to collect your dessert from our wonderful cooks, Mrs Platt and Miss Mason. Be sure to thank them for all their hard work. No doubt your taste buds are in for a tantalising treat!!" he beamed.

Was he actually serious?

I nudged Edna, "Who is that man?" I was so confused. "What is that he is doing?" I asked before she could reply to my first question.

"That's Mr Flatley, the Deputy Head," she answered, "he's a crazy, Irish dancing maniac!"

"I've never seen anything like it!" I said. "Is that normal for him to go off like that? Are those legs actually attached to his body?"

Edna sniggered, "You'll get used to it. He does it all day, every day!!"

He says he's ***the*** Michael Flatley's cousin."

"Really?" I asked, pretending I knew who that was.

"Yeah, he always talks about them growing up together, going to competitions and stuff," said Edna, "but I'm not sure it's true."

"Ohhh," was all I could muster in response.

I couldn't wait to get home to google who this Michael man was.

Before long, we were up at the counter, face-to-face with Mrs Platt and her ginormous saucepan of lumpy, clumpy, curdled custard. Dangling the ladle in front of me, the plump, frizzy, red-haired lady examined me. Luckily, I sighed silently, she couldn't see below my waist.

"And what's your name?" she asked, still inspecting every freckle on my face.

There were a few beads of sweat about to drip from her forehead, but she caught them with a tea towel. I wondered how many drips had landed into the large pot of custard delight.

I felt nauseous at the stench and sight of the gurgling, bright yellow liquid.

"Felicity," I said, smiling tentatively.

"Good to meet a new face, sweetheart. Mrs Platt, I am," she replied. "Custard for your cake?"

"Emm," I hesitated, "I don't really like custard."

I sensed this was her pride and joy, and my heart raced in anticipation for her response. I didn't have to wait too long.

"Sorry? You don't want custard! How can you *not like* custard?" she asked, staring at me, absolutely gobsmacked.

Before I could reply, she was off on a rant.

"I mean, it's one of the nicest desserts in the world! You haven't tasted mine yet... I mean, mine is renowned about these parts. Renowned, I tell you! Any time there's a funeral mass or an event in the parish hall, 'Get the custard on the pot I'm told, Petunia, the town needs you, the town needs you to work your magic.' I mean, Father Brennan says my custard creation is the best in the county. Sure, when the bishop came..."

"I'll take some then, please," I interrupted abruptly, in the hope of putting an end to the manic custard conversation and all the babbling.

"You make sure you let me know what you think of it afterwards."

My heart sank to the pit of my stomach. By the width of the smile spread across her face, I genuinely felt my acceptance of her finest clotted custard recipe had made Mrs Platt's heart happy. I also felt sure that saying no to it would *never ever* be an option.

Back down at the table, I knew I only had one hope. I passed my bowl subtly to Jenny. From the counter, I could feel Mrs Platt's eyes peering down on me. I snatched the bowl back, slowly scooped up the smallest amount of the lumpy liquid in my spoon and forced it into my mouth. It was as grotesque as I'd predicted. Think of the worst thing you have ever tasted and multiply it by about 45; that might give you an accurate idea of how bad it was!

I smiled as much as I could manage and nodded up towards Mrs Platt, who had been distracted by a child in front of her - no doubt also being force-fed. I still had the liquid in my mouth, and I gulped it down with a swig of water, the lumps catching the back of my throat. I was heaving. I was really annoyed that she'd missed seeing me actually manage to get a spoonful down my gullet without retching out loud.

I continued with my plan. I hid behind Jenny, whose wide back faced away from the dynamic dinner lady. I grabbed an empty spoon and made scooping movements like I was eating. I slowly pushed the bowl back towards Jenny. She certainly knew how to be crafty with food and was soon eating the contents without anyone noticing; she was very fast and carefully-skilled.

As I went to line up to go outside, I awkwardly gave Mrs Platt a thumbs up. She smiled and gave me a double thumbs up in return. I really hoped no one had seen this exchange between us.

"Jenny," I said, as I stood behind her in the line, "you saved me there, thank you. I just couldn't..."

"Any time," she replied. "Sure, I just love custard. I just love Tuesday Treat Day... I just love food in general. All types," she giggled.

CHAPTER 3

TERRIBLE TRIO

After my first dining room ordeal, I walked to the playground with Edna. We didn't talk about going together; it just kind of happened. Sienna Sorski was tagging along behind, and I couldn't help but feel sorry for her. No one seemed to give her any attention at all. I turned around and wagged at her to walk faster and join us.

"What do you usually do at breaktime?" I asked awkwardly as she sauntered along beside me. I couldn't think of one other thing to ask her.

To me, she looked either alarmed or disgusted at my question. I didn't know her well enough to work out what each of her scowl variations meant.

"Me?" she asked.

I nodded, "Yes, well... St. Bernadette's pupils."

"I don't like any of the games they play out here. I usually just count down the seconds until we are back inside again, into the heat. I mean, this freezing Irish weather. I hate it!"

"What *don't* you hate?" Edna butted in.

Seeming to ignore Edna or pretend she didn't hear her (again, I was confused), Sienna continued, "I just can't wait to go back to the warm weather in Dubai in the summer. We have a yacht, and it's beautiful there."

I grinned at her, pretending I knew where Dubai was. Suddenly, I felt less sorry for her.

Martha Molloy appeared behind us, munching very loudly on a Cadbury's Crunchie.

"Sienna," she interrupted, with sticky honeycomb smeared all over her front teeth. I had the feeling she knew this but just didn't care.

"Yeah, Martha?" Sienna asked, open-mouthed and with raised eyebrows, like she knew nothing kind was going to come from her mouth.

"You'd make more friends, you know, if you stopped boasting so much."

Changing her voice to a whine, Martha continued, "UGH, I hate my life, I hate Ireland, I hate my pony, my pool, my yacht, this weather, mindfulness, blah, blah, blah, blah, blah, blah, blah!"

She gave her a fairly good list, I thought.

Sienna's chin began to tremble violently.

"I never say I hate my pony!"

"Well, that must be the only thing you don't yap on about then!" said a very matter-of-fact Martha Molly.

I didn't want to be involved, so I began to scan the playground of children playing either football, basketball or tag.

"You're always yapping about something, your three swimming pools or something... I'm not trying to be mean," said Martha, perhaps realising she had gone too far. "I'm just trying to tell you that it's annoying to listen to."

"I only have one! One swimming pool!" Sienna snapped, fixating on this rather than Martha's last comment. She was biting on her lip to stop the tears.

At that moment, I noticed three blonde girls strutting across the yard towards us. They were flicking their hair in time as they went. The group immediately went silent, and we all stared at them. I gasped, noticing as they came closer that the three of them looked identical to one another. They had the exact same tight, curly mops of golden hair. Irresistible heads of hair, obviously, as they couldn't keep their hands off them.

Their locks were embellished with T-initial hair pins and they wore long, white socks and wide, over-the-knee school skirts.

"Oh, here we go," Edna rolled her eyes.

The three girls pranced at speed through the games of basketball like they owned the whole school and its grounds.

Martha whispered to me, "The Turner triplets."

That explains it.

The three of them now stood about two metres in front of us, gawking, with their hands on their hips. They even stood in the same position; the one in the middle was slightly taller than her comrades on either side of her.

"Who's the new girl?" said the obvious chief and tallest of the three.

I instantly stepped backwards, wanting to hide away. Edna impetuously stood

in front of me.

"Felicity is her name! Why, what's it to you what her name is?" she asked, eyeballing each of them in turn.

The three girls, in sync, tutted and sighed.

"Excuse me!" said the one on the right.

"You're excused!" Martha butted in.

"Oh my goodness... What are those? asked the middle triplet, her voice pitched like a witch's shriek. She pointed at my feet.

"What are those?" the other two triplets repeated in time with each other.

The three of them began to cackle loudly. Cackles that pierced your ears until they rang in pain. I was shaking with embarrassment and could feel my neck start to burn its usual shade of crimson red.

Suddenly, out of nowhere, Jenny Jackson lunged in front of the terrible trio, blocking full sight of them from the rest of the group with her broad back.

"Do you know what?" Jenny asked them.

"What?" asked the first triplet sarcastically.

"What?" repeated the second and third triplets together.

"*What?*" Jenny mocked.

The rest of the group split to each side of Jenny's body to be able to see what was going on.

"I actually feel really, really sorry for you three," said Jenny, pointing at them, her left hand firmly placed on her hip.

"Especially you two!" she added, looking at the triplets on the outside.

"You both stand there repeating exactly everything she says, echoing behind her all the time, following your leader!"

"They do not!" protested the median one.

"Oh, but they do!" answered Jenny. "It must be awful being bullied by your own sister, is it not?" she asked the one on the left.

The triplet stammered, "Emm... Em... she does not bully me! She..."

Jenny interrupted, "I think you three pests should go back to the other side of the playground before I slam dunk each one of you into the Atlantic Ocean. At the same time, of course. Wouldn't want to separate you from each other," she chortled.

I laughed nervously, in disbelief at what was happening. The other girls in our group erupted into screeches of laughter. Martha was smacking her legs, roaring in amusement at what Jenny had just said. Edna laughed like it was the best thing she'd seen all year. Sienna didn't smile much.

"You can't tell us what to do!" shouted the bossy one.

"You can't tell us what to do!" copied the other two (yes, at exactly the same time).

As if realising that what Jenny had just said was actually true, the three of them suddenly looked very awkward.

"Listen," said Edna, "Great Auntie Bog Breath can't always save you."

"How dare you speak to us like that!" yelled the middle triplet as she marched away from us towards the school building, with her two little ducks following closely behind her.

Later that day, Miss Green announced we would be having a visit from Mr Flatley before home time. I was glad she had warned us because, although I was startled at the clip-clapping sound initially, I quickly realised the noise that enveloped the classroom at around 2.30 pm was Mr Maniac Modern Dancer making an appearance. I was baffled at how the others in the class didn't even flinch when the loud tap-athon started.

He clip-clapped from the doorway to the front of the classroom, legs flinging this time at about fifty miles per hour from the ground to the air and back again. It was hard to follow; he was so fast on his feet. Edna and I shared a look. She knew what I was thinking.

I had never witnessed the speed of human movement like it in my life. How he managed to move so quickly and still be able to breathe, I did not know. I was mesmerised by him but tried hard to hide it. I wasn't sure if this style of dancing was cool, and I'd certainly never seen a teacher behave like this before, randomly, in the middle of a classroom or dining room. He *was* very intriguing, though.

"Right, folks! I have some exciting news!" he announced.

"Very exciting news," added Miss Green with a wide, enthusiastic grin.

"Yes, Miss Green!" replied Mr Flatley hastily.

"We are delighted to announce that our Irish dancing after-school club is reopening next week. The Contemporary Celts! Well, we are back!"

"The what?" I mouthed to Edna.

She giggled.

"I would be *so* happy if as many children in this class as possible signed up for the club. You don't need any experience; we accept beginners! I will teach you, literally step-by-step, everything you need to know to become an Irish dancing sensation, just like myself. Well... almost as sensational as me."

"Irish dancing is therapeutic and good for the mind, body and soul," smiled Miss Green, displaying her twinkling gnashers.

"Could I do it, too?" asked Jenny Jackson.

"Certainly!" answered Miss Green passionately. "Why would you not be able to do it? I have no doubt you would have a lot to offer. You *all* would!" she said, looking around at the sea of unenthused heads.

"Miss, can you dance a jig for us now?" asked Billy Barlow.

"I'm afraid we don't have the time for that now, Billy," interrupted Mr Flatley. "Maybe another time," he said through gritted teeth.

Clearly disappointed, Miss Green added, "I'll happily join your class one afternoon and dance with you all."

"Back to my point," said Mr Flatley, wagging parental permission forms above his head.

Edna nudged me, "I will if you will," she said eagerly.

I was shocked she was even slightly interested. "Me?" I answered. "I couldn't; I don't know anything about it."

"Of course you could," she replied. "Jenny's doing it," she added, pointing her head towards her.

Meanwhile, Jenny was jumping out of her seat to grab a form.

"I'll do it, Sir, I'll do it!" she roared. "I'll become a dancing sensation, too!"

Mr Flatley handed her the sheet of paper. "Well, if we're not in, we can't win," he said.

"Okay," I whispered to Edna, slowly putting my hand in the air. I guessed it was a good way to try to get to know people. And, secretly, I wanted to see Mr Flatley's dance routines.

"Felicity," said Miss Green ecstatically, "I think you are going to really love Irish dancing!"

I half-nodded, wishing my teacher knew exactly how much I hated being in the spotlight.

"You *are* actually going to love it," Martha told me.

"Hmm," I replied, unconvinced. Watching it, perhaps, I thought, but I wasn't so sure about the taking part bit.

Bog Breath suddenly appeared at the door, asking to speak to Jenny.

What could the dreadful boss of the school want her for, I wondered.

I suddenly remembered the antics in the playground. *Ohhhhh noooooooo...*

Miss Green was instantly defensive. "What is this about?" she asked Bowman.

"An incident from earlier today!" hissed the hideous headteacher, her slithering, snaking tongue peeking from its home in her mouth.

My heart started to thud violently.

"Those nasty nieces of yours, they started it!" Jenny protested.

Bog Breath's eyes bulged from their sockets, her glasses steamed up and a scarlet mist surrounded the top part of her wrinkly body.

She walked towards where Jenny was sitting, spitting as she went.

"Jennifer Jackson, never respond to me OR refer to the Turner girls like that again! Do you hear me?"

Jenny showed no fear at all.

"Now, up on your feet and into my office at once!" she demanded, pointing her stick towards the door.

"I'll come with Jenny," said Miss Green assertively.

Bowman was furious. "Indeed you will not! There is no such need!"

"I think you'll find there is," added Miss Green, walking towards the door behind them.

"Mr Flatley, please dismiss the class today," she called over to him, leaving neither him nor Ms Bowman with any choice in the matter.

A few minutes later, just as we were packing our belongings away for home, Miss Green put her head through the classroom door and asked Edna, Martha, Sienna and me to join her at Ms Bowman's office. Before long, we were outside the office door and being called in one by one to speak to the two teachers about the playground incident. I was the first one up and my knees knocked against each other as I awaited my interrogation.

"So sorry," I mouthed to Jenny as she left the office, and I made my way into the dreaded lion's den.

"I'm not bothered! I *would* slam dunk them if they started again!" she chuckled loudly as she made her way up the corridor towards the classroom. "The bottom of the ocean would be too good for those three!"

Inside the office, Bowman was sitting at her desk. She hadn't got hold of the WD stuff (or the caretaker hadn't) by the sounds of the creaking chair. Miss Green was pacing up and down the room.

"Please, take a seat," ordered the horrible headmistress.

I hesitantly sat down opposite her, my eyes focused on that slithery tongue of hers, rolling around in that ghastly mouth.

"It is such a shame that, on your first day here, we had to learn there was an incident out in the playground."

I nodded, "Yes, but..."

"But," she interrupted, "my great-nieces... the Turner triplets," she corrected herself, "informed me that they only asked why you were able to wear shoes that aren't part of the school uniform."

"That's not true!" I answered sharply.

"You will have your turn to speak, Felicity, don't worry," said Miss Green, gently tapping me on the arm.

"They advised they approached you in a friendly manner, asking about your shoes and that Jenny Jackson, out of nowhere, told them she was going to slam dunk them, very specifically into the Atlantic Ocean. Slam dunk of all things! I mean, what even is a slam dunk?" She looked baffled.

"It's a basketball shot," Miss Green informed her sarcastically.

"Basketball shot?" Bowman asked, open-mouthed.

Miss Green ignored her, taking a seat beside me, "Is this what happened?" she asked.

"No," I replied, my eyes now fixated on the floor.

"The girls don't tend to tell lies!" exclaimed Bog Breath.

"Ms Bowman, you need to let Felicity speak," retorted Miss Green.

I was beginning to feel a lot less happy about my first day at St. Bernadette's.

"Felicity, don't be afraid to tell us; you need to be able to tell your version of events," said the kind teacher.

I looked up at the two of them for a second but then focused my eyes out the window.

"I, I..." I stammered, "was standing with the girls..."

"Edna, Jenny, Sienna and...?" asked Miss Green.

"I think we have already established who was there at the time," interjected the beastly Bowman.

"Yes," I replied, "Jenny wasn't there, though, at the beginning. She came along all of a sudden and stood in front of us when the girls were trying to embarrass me about my shoes."

"What do you mean *embarrass* you?" exclaimed Bowman. "They were only asking why you were allowed to wear them, you mean?"

"No, they didn't ask; they pointed at them! They didn't ask anything about why I was allowed to wear them. They were laughing at them."

"I don't think pointing at shoes is a big issue, Felicity," said Bowman.

"What do you mean?" inquired Miss Green, staring at me again, ignoring her boss.

I told her how they pointed and laughed.

"And how did this make you feel?" she asked, with concern in her eyes.

"Really embarrassed," I answered. "They were trying to make a big deal of them and make a fool out of me."

"With all due respect, your shoes are not part of the school uniform," added Ms Bowman.

Wafts of her putrid breath flew across the table.

"We have discussed this, Ms Bowman," snapped Miss Green.

"How inappropriate!!"

She. Was. Fuming.

"Felicity, thank you for coming in and telling us what happened," said Miss Green, a few seconds later, when her rage had settled a little.

"Rest assured, you had every right to feel embarrassed at that moment, and I can tell you that this is not okay. What I would ask is that if anything happens like this again, you always inform a trusted adult, straight away if you can, to help resolve the situation."

"I will," I half-grinned back at her. I knew she believed me.

"And as for your flipflops," she added, glaring as she spoke at Bowman, like she was chastising a small child, "you ARE allowed to wear them in this school and make sure you continue to. They are a part of you."

"I will," I replied as I stood up to leave. I sighed with relief.

On the later bus journey home, Edna filled me in.

"We didn't even have to go in to speak to them in the end. We were able to listen in on the chat between them."

"Really?" I asked.

"Wouldn't say it was a chat actually, more like a screaming match. I'd be surprised if Father Brennan didn't hear them in the parish hall."

"Why? What were they saying?"

"It was mostly led by Miss Green. She was so angry! I've never heard her go off like that before!"

"What did she say?"

"Emm," she hesitated, "I'll be honest with you, she was ranting something about you being a looked-after child and the shoes being part of a package or a care plan or something."

I wanted to get off the bus. Immediately.

"I don't even know what that means," she tried to reassure me. "Neither do the others."

"I... I...," I stammered. "It means..."

"You don't have to explain..."

"It's okay," I replied. "It means I'm in foster care."

"Ahhh," nodded Edna, intently. "I don't mean to sound nosey; I was just being honest about what was said."

"I know that...it means I don't live with my parents... They couldn't look after me, so that's why I live with Bella."

"I see," said Edna. She was struggling to elaborate.

"It's okay," I answered, fidgeting with my fingernails. "I love living with Bella."

"Cool," she said.

"The flipflops," I continued. "I've worn them since I was a small child. They kind of... emm... mean a lot to me... I've had to have them altered to fit me a few times. I don't really wear anything else."

"Ah, I see..." replied Edna.

"I sound crazy."

"Crazy?" she asked.

"Yes," I answered.

"If you're crazy, not sure what that makes me... I am a girl who likes boys' clothes and short haircuts."

"What's wrong with that?" I asked.

"Well... if this makes you feel any better... I *do* actually live with both my parents, and they have no idea of anything about me. My mum has already picked me out a sparkly dress for my cousin's wedding next summer," she tittered.

"Well, I think you look great as you are..." I replied, trying to sound semi-cool and confident.

"You're right, I do.... Thank you," she replied, fixing her shirt collar.

"I get the feeling that me and you are going to get on well," she smiled at me.

"Me too," I replied awkwardly, "and thank you for sticking up for me today."

"Oh, against the twisted triplets! We always have fights with them. They're nothing but bullies."

We sat in comfortable silence the rest of the journey home.

CHAPTER 4.

DRESSMAKING DISTRESS

"....and they laughed at my flipflops," I said, sitting at the table munching my favourite thick-based margherita pizza, curly fries and mayonnaise with Bella.

"I'll be going into that school to sort them three out! And that awful excuse for a headteacher!" Bella exclaimed.

"It's okay," I reassured her.

I told her about Jenny's threats, in between chuckles.

Bella laughed, "Oh, I do like the sound of this Jenny girl."

"Yeah, they're all nice. Well, obviously, apart from those terrible triplets. Sienna Sorski is a moan, but I feel a bit sorry for her, *sometimes.*"

"Why?"

"Her mum and dad are never home really... always working away."

"I see," said Bella. "Does she have any siblings?"

"I don't think so," I replied. "None that she talks about anyway."

"She must get a bit lonely," said Bella.

"Yeah, I suppose she does," I replied.

I certainly knew how that felt sometimes.

"Anything else exciting happen today?" she asked.

I decided not to tell her about the office scenario. For now. I remembered my permission form.

"I signed up for an Irish dancing after-school club," I told her.

"Wow," Bella beamed, "that's fantastic! It will really help build your confidence."

I hesitated. "Maybe... I suppose it'll help me make new friends."

Dawn M. Gelston

"Have you ever tried Irish dancing before?"

"No," I answered. "I have no idea about it."

"You could be a pro before you know it," said Bella reassuringly.

"Not with these awkward feet," I joked, pointing towards my toes.

"I can make you a pair of pumps."

"Pumps?" I asked. I had no idea what she meant.

"Irish dancing pumps... you know... you will probably start off in them... They're a little bit like ballerina pumps."

"Oh, okay," I answered.

The only footwear I was ever used to wearing were these flipflops and the latest, warmer version Bella had made of them for me.

Perhaps after today's events, it was time to take the jump and get used to wearing something different. Even just sometimes. I felt extremely nervous about the thought of that, though. They were my *happy place*, and, as Miss Green reminded me earlier, they were a part of me.

"I will definitely make you a dress anyway!" said Bella excitedly.

"A dress?" I asked.

"Yes, sure, the Irish dancing costumes are so stunning...so much detail in them."

I smiled at her, wanting to please her, "That would be nice."

Getting Edna into one of them might be a bit of a challenge, I giggled to myself.

Later that evening, I was in my bedroom googling Michael Flatley on my iPad when I heard screaming and shouting coming from Bella's sewing room below.

"What am I going to do now?" roared a high-pitched, unfamiliar voice. It must be the bride in for a fitting Bella had told me about, I remembered.

I could hear Bella trying to reassure her calmly.

"Listen, I can slot a new piece of material in; you won't even be able to notice."

"Won't be able to notice?" the woman screeched. "My dress is about five inches too small and doesn't go halfway around my waist! How will it not be noticed? Tell me!!" she demanded.

"Well, with respect, Donna, I measured you accurately at the last fitting."

"Are you saying I've put on weight?" she yelled at her.

"Well, why else would it not fit?" sniped Bella. "The material is incapable of shrinking, and the dress fitted you perfectly six weeks ago."

"Oh my goodness!!" the irate woman wailed. "I have! I have! I have put on weight, haven't I?" she asked, in a softer tone, as if suddenly admitting defeat.

"Yes," answered Bella, "you have put on a little bit of weight."

"What am I going to do? The wedding is next Friday! Liposuction? Do you think that would work?" she asked hysterically.

"Donna, let me show you what I'll do. I'll take the dress out here," Bella said, "and add in a little bit more taffeta."

"Right, right, right. Okay!!! You don't think I need lipo then?"

"No," sighed Bella.

The noise level below turned to mumbles, but a couple of minutes later, Bella was shouting up the stairs for me to come down to help her. I sprinted downstairs and into the sewing room. The hysterical woman, who I'd gathered was called Donna, was stuck in her wedding dress and was sobbing. Bella was carefully trying to peel it off her over her head without it ripping.

"Felicity," said Bella calmly, "I need you to come to the other side and help me take this off... pull it really gently and slowly over Donna's head."

"It's not going to come off without tearing!" screeched the frantic bride-to-be. "It's ruined! My day is going to be ruined! I don't need this! I don't need it!" she cried dramatically.

"Your day isn't going to be ruined," said Bella, irritated. "We'll get you out of it. You just need to stay very still and calm down. And be quiet!" she said firmly.

The woman gasped in shock at being scolded.

Bella winked at me as I held the top part of the glitzy gown, ready to help her out of this pressurised predicament. I was trying my best not to laugh out loud.

"When I tell you, Donna, I need you to breathe in as tight as you can, and me and Felicity will get it off you, once and for all, okay?"

"Yes," she replied in a child-like manner.

The stressed seamstress nodded at me.

"Ready, Felicity? On the count of three, breathe in Donna... One, two, three."

In perfect timing, my foster mum and I, through nervous shakes and sweaty palms, managed to sweep the dress from over the distressed woman's head without her back bursting through the zip.

"Thank you, thank you!" she yelled, hugging Bella and me in turn, as tight as she could to show her over-dramatic appreciation. I thought she was going to crush my ribcage.

"Bella, I am sorry! So sorry!" she repeated. "I have been over-eating, with nerves, I think, in the run-up to the wedding day. I think I've just been in denial. I have been eating cake for breakfast some mornings and McDonald's takeaways most evenings.

I can never get my stomach filled if I'm honest."

"Donna, don't worry... it happens. Lots of us eat more when we're stressed."

'You can sort the dress, though, can't you? With the extra taffeta?"

"Yes," Bella reassured her AGAIN. "Give me a few days, and I will have it sorted."

"I will buy you something amazing for this, I promise."

After the tear-stained face of Donna had left, Bella and I plonked like heavy weights on top of the sofa.

"I've never seen a woman like that in my life before!" I giggled.

"Yeah, she's one of a kind, alright! Constantly eats cake for breakfast and Maccy-Ds dinners and can't understand why she nearly ruptured her spleen getting out of her wedding dress. A dress that used to fit her perfectly, might I add," chuckled Bella.

CHAPTER 5

MONDAY MORNING MASS

First thing after registration on Monday morning, we embarked on our walk to the chapel beside the school building. It was my first outing to school mass at St. Bernadette's Chapel. It was a cold, frosty morning, and the wind nipped my toes and hands. I was glad to be on the inside of the line, shielded slightly from the bitter sea wind by Edna, who I was pleased to have been paired with again.

I had not been to a mass in years. I knew my grandparents used to take me on a Saturday evening when I was very young, but I had very vague memories of it. Edna had told me not to worry and just to follow the lead of everyone else when it came to standing up and sitting down at certain times during the service.

Before departing, Miss Green had looked very serious and had warned all twenty-seven of us not to make as much as a squeak of a sound for the whole duration of our time in the religious building.

Bowman had been leading the lines of upper school children walking the short distance and was approaching us at speed, swinging her stick as usual.

"Fingers on your lips!" she demanded, holding her crooked, pencil-thin fingers against her own. "Remember, you are the oldest children in the school and need to act as positive role models for the younger pupils!"

A waft of her stinky, sewer breath made its way down the line of children now stopped in their tracks, shivering in the early-morning cold.

Miss Green shook her head in disbelief, "You've no worries here," she replied. "6A's behaviour is always impeccable! They are always excellent representatives of the school, aren't you children?" she smiled at us, with a glint in her eyes which warned us not to even think about letting her down.

"Hmm, is that so?" asked Bowman, marching towards the end of our line, pointing her walking stick towards the twins, Alan and Adam Adamson, who were caught up in a row over Gaelic football scores, and completely oblivious to her presence beside them.

"These two seem to be displaying impeccable behaviour, don't they?" she asked, smugly, before strutting off towards the next line. It was obvious she was intent on picking on our class teacher at any opportunity, and Miss Green, understandably, did not like this one bit.

The annoyed teacher made her way to the boys within about two seconds.

"Enough of the chatting boys!" she grimaced. "Adam, up to the front of the line now, please!"

Adam, a usually-chirpy, brown-haired boy, sighed and slowly began to make his way to the top of the line.

"Always me," he muttered. "Alan always gets off with it."

"I heard that," replied Miss Green, "we can chat about this back at school later," she told him as she ushered us all to walk faster towards the chapel.

Inside the 200-year-old building, we were seated in the front two rows, still annoyingly being forced to keep our fingers tightly pressed against our lips. My right arm was already starting to ache.

I glanced around at the statues of Our Lady and Jesus, the chalices and the baptismal font, wondering what they all actually stood for. There were huge, intricate, stained-glass windows behind the altar. I was trying to work out what the picture of Jesus carrying a cross on one of them meant when Mrs Rodgers startled me. Yet again. She had suddenly appeared in front of the altar, sssshing everyone and clicking her fingers around in the air dramatically. As far as I could see, every child in attendance had followed the strict instructions to barely breathe, and you could almost hear a pin drop in the dead silence inside the large, echoey building. What a waste of her energy, I thought.

A few seconds later, the frantic finger-clicker scarpered off to her seat and Father Brennan arrived on the altar with two altar boys. Immediately, the whole crowd stood up, led by Bog Breath at the front. Everyone, and I mean *everyone*, including each of my classmates, began singing a song about 'having joy in their hearts,' very, very, very, very badly.

Awkwardly, I stood among the rows of strangled cats attempting to sing at the top of their voices, actually praying (with my hands clasped together) for it to be over. The priest joined in and drowned out some of the screeching blares; I was surprised to hear he had a strong, although sometimes quaking, semi-bearable voice.

"Hopefully, it's a short one today," Martha whispered beside me when the feline-choking session was finally over. I nodded, scared of being rumbled by Mrs Rodgers.

I was actually very shocked to find the mass was a very calming experience. I had heard adults go on about it before.

Adult Quote: "Mass is a time to feel close to God and a time to reflect and appreciate all the good things we have..."

I didn't feel overly close to God as yet, but I was enjoying the peacefulness. I was, more importantly, happy to be out of lessons. What a bonus.

After the second reading was read by a nervous, stammering boy from Year Five, Father Brennan started to say another prayer I was unfamiliar with.

I looked across at the rows of pupils on the other side of the chapel and spotted the terrible trio, sitting with their heads arched to the right, in the exact same position, of course.

Ms Bowman was perched on the very front row on the right side of the chapel. Alone. I wondered if being on her own was normal for her and whether she had any family. I knew she had the triplets for great-nieces, but I was curious to know if she had any children of her own. I decided this was very unlikely as she appeared to detest children. You could say she hated the actual sight of them.

Father Brennan stood a short while later with the chalice in his hand, preparing for Holy Communion (Edna had quietly informed me). I had never made the sacrament of First Holy Communion, I suddenly remembered, which meant I couldn't go to the front to receive this with the rest of the school when the time came. My palms began to sweat. Typical. *What was I going to do? Could I just go up and bluff and blag my way through it?*

The priest talked about the circular bread he held out in front of him being the 'body of Christ.' I was completely puzzled at how he had worked this out. He bit into the bread slowly and began to swallow.

All of a sudden, Father Brennan began grasping and pulling at his throat and neck. His eyes started to bulge from their sockets, and his face rapidly changed to deep red and then a dark shade of purple.

Before I knew it, I was standing behind him, pushing him forward and patting him hard repeatedly between his shoulder blades with the heel of my hand. On the fifth blow, the piece of bread shot from his mouth, across the air and right onto the left lens of beastly Bowman's glasses. The whole building gasped in disbelief. Bowman shot up out of her seat, shaking the soggy bread off her beloved spectacles and it hit the ground. She looked like she was going to spew everywhere.

I stood in complete and utter shock. I couldn't even remember getting to the front of the chapel and past all the other children seated beside me. That part was a blinding blur. Miss Green was standing beside Father Brennan, reassuring him that he was going to be okay.

The shaking priest, recovering his breath slightly, tapped me on the shoulder and, struggling, managed to say the words *"Thank you, my child,"* before being escorted by the PE teacher, Mr Magee, into the room at the back of the chapel to recover from the incident.

A swarm of heads quickly surrounded me at the front of the building. It was my class, welcomed to huddle around and high-five me by Miss Green.

"You are an amazing young lady!" exclaimed the ecstatic teacher.

"Well done, Felicity!" roared Billy Barlow, patting me on the back, much too hard. I'm sure it was almost as hard as I had just been striking the priest.

I don't ever remember a time when I was as embarrassed in my whole eleven years and five months of life. Awkwardly, I fixed my eyes on the dark green carpet, begging for it all to be over.

Ms Bowman made her way to the altar and stared at our happy teacher, horrified.

"Right, enough of that!" she yelled at us. "Back to school at once! This is God's house, Miss Green!"

She looked at her like she was a wart on her wrinkly, wretched neck.

"The child has just saved Father Brennan's life! I think she deserves at least a few moments of credit from her friends. On this occasion, I think God himself would agree!" Miss Green hissed back at her.

Bog Breath turned on her heels, and her and her hunched-back made their way down the aisle, screeching at the rest of the mass attendees to line up instantly and head back towards the school building.

The hype from the choking incident continued throughout the school day. At lunchtime, children constantly approached me, praising me for what I had done for the school priest earlier that day.

Edna smiled at me delightedly, "Only here a few days and a bit of a celeb already."

"I don't think so," I smiled back at her, embarrassed.

I was beginning to feel a little proud of my actions in helping the choking priest, but wasn't well-receiving of the aftermath of attention from so many people.

"Role modelling," beamed Miss Green. "You couldn't get better role modelling than that, Felicity; you should be so proud of yourself," she told me as I was leaving the classroom for the bus home.

"Thanks," I managed to respond, my eyes still concentrated on the cold, tiled floor.

Later that day, Bella and I walked along the beach, paddling our feet in the icy, numbing water. It was freezing, but bliss. The sun was getting ready to go to bed for the night, and I looked out towards the majestic, misty Atlantic Ocean, thinking about the day's events. It was hard to forget them when they'd been the focus of *everything* at school all day. After Bella received a phone call from Miss Green sharing the events during mass, she had been ecstatic, too. Over. The. Moon.

"How did you know what to do today?" she asked me, her voice full of curiosity.

I hesitated.

"You don't have to speak about it if you don't want to," smiled Bella.

She did know me so well.

"No, it's okay," I replied, clearing my throat. "When I lived with my Grandad, he had a stroke. Afterwards, his swallow was never the same, so my Gran and I were trained in first aid: how to save him if he choked."

"Ah, I see," nodded Bella. "It's amazing that you knew exactly what to do and to act so quickly."

"I guess so," I replied, not really thinking of it in any other way than something I'd been trained to do.

"He choked a couple of times, and I was able to help him," I replied nonchalantly. "Luckily," I added.

"Luckily is right," said Bella. "Very lucky for Father Brennan today, too."

I felt content with Bella and that I could trust her, so I decided to share a little more with her.

"When I used to see a psychologist, he used to talk about how people can respond to a stressful situation or trauma... like it being a fight, flight or freeze reaction type of thing. We found out I was a fight-type of reactor. Well...sometimes. In some situations, I might freeze on the spot, though. Like when the triplets started to laugh at me, I couldn't really defend myself."

"Yes, but you have the fighting spirit," added Bella. "You can stand up to them."

"Maybe one day, but today... I really don't even remember how I made it there so quickly. It's so blurry."

"Instinctive," replied Bella, hugging me. "Sometimes we just act; adrenaline kicks in, and that's it."

I nodded in agreement, sort of understanding what she meant.

"You really are a fantastic, mature young lady, Felicity," she said. "Someday, we'll get you actually starting to believe it!"

"Mmm... maybe," I smiled back at her, feeling less embarrassed than I usually would.

CHAPTER 6

FOOT FLINGS AND FEELINGS

The next day at school, after all the lessons were done for the day, the twenty-seven of us were again sprawled on the heavenly, snug bean bags on the floor of the classroom. As usual, Jenny was fighting the urge to sleep, and Sienna's face was twisted like a screwed-up crisp packet. She never *ever* seemed to be happy.

Billy had a mischievous twinkle in his eye and threw a ruler over towards one of the Adamson twins, hitting him on the leg (Alan, I thought—it was always difficult to tell).

"What do you want?" whispered the twin towards him.

It wasn't long before Billy was caught.

"Billy!" exclaimed Miss 'Doesn't-Miss-A-Trick' Green. "That could have really hurt Adam!"

I was wrong.

"Sorry, Miss, I didn't throw it hard... I... I...," he muttered. "I was just wanting to ask him if he was going to football training later."

"Save the football chat for after school, please," she said, as cool as a cucumber.

She then held up a large, painted, leafless tree and started to pin it against a sad-looking display board at the front of the classroom.

"This," she announced, pointing at it and seeming pleased with her artistic efforts, "is our new *tree of feelings*..."

"What's that?" asked Billy, smiling at her enthusiastically, eager to get into her good books again. 'Mr Goody-Two-Shoes' as usual.

"We will be putting a wide variety of feelings on this tree. On its leaves! These will be the feelings of us ALL in 6A. But, first of all, we need to come up with some typical feelings."

I wasn't sure where she was going with this, exactly.

She took a pile of empty green leaves from a tray and held one up.

"I want each of you to suggest a feeling for our tree... not just positive feelings, negative ones too. Remember, we all have our bad days, and our feelings can change very quickly from positive to negative or the other way round within a short time. There are many different types of feelings."

I certainly agreed with that.

She scanned the room.

"Right, who's going to go first?" she asked.

I had knots in my stomach, and, as always, my hands began to sweat at the mere thought of speaking out.

"Felicity, let's start with you...what do you think?" I was shaking and stared down at my feet. N-I-G-H-T-M-A-R-E.

"I'll give you a hint... how did you feel after yesterday's incident in the chapel?"

I couldn't manage a reply. My breathing quickened. My mouth would just not open.

"Begins with a P," she hinted.

I knew what it was, but I just couldn't bear to bring myself to speak. To say that one measly word.

"How about I write it for you?" she suggested, beginning to scribble down on the leaf.

"Proud!" she beamed when she had finished scrolling.

She held it up high for all to see.

"A lovely feeling we have when we do something for another person, or have produced a piece of work we have put a lot of effort into. For example, you, I hope, are feeling very proud of what you did yesterday!"

I just wanted her to stop talking to me.

After going around the room for at least twenty torturous minutes, we now had around fifty leaves of feelings pinned onto the tree. Some children had offered two, even three ideas.

Meanwhile, I was still recovering from the embarrassment of not being able to answer out in class. At all. Again.

I cursed myself for not managing to say anything. Not even one five-letter word. I had never even heard of some of the feelings the class had come up with, but soon learnt the meaning of them thanks to some of my peers' informative, detailed explanations.

Here is a list of some of them:

PROUD	DELIGHTED
CALM	ECSTATIC
CONTENT	DISCOMBOBULATED (Sienna's effort)
DISTRACTED	THRILLED
RELAXED	PREOCCUPIED
FRUSTRATED	FEARLESS
ANGRY	CHILLED
EMBARRASSED	JEALOUS
NERVOUS	IRRITATED
ANXIOUS	ANNOYED
HAPPY	PANICKED
EXCITED	ENTHRALLED
RELIEVED	ENTHUSIASTIC
CONFIDENT	SELF-CONSCIOUS
DETERMINED	DEVASTATED
UNHAPPY	POSITIVE
UPBEAT	SATISFIED
PLEASED	BAFFLED
BEWILDERED	CONFUSED
CAUTIOUS	WEARY
WARY	TIRED (PHYSICAL FEELING)
GLAD	SUCCESSFUL
ACCOMPLISHED	BEMUSED
AMUSED	APPREHENSIVE

Miss Green picked out the *delighted* feeling to describe how she felt at the end of the day with everyone's efforts to cover the once-leafless tree with a mixture of new, leaved-feelings. She ended the conversation with a reminder to us all of the importance of being able to acknowledge and discuss how we are feeling and to take on board and be aware of the feelings of others.

Suddenly, I began to feel less comfortable about being in the 6A class. I had always struggled to talk about my feelings, speak out in class and, admittedly, consider the feelings of others.

Unfortunately, it looked like there was no way out of it. Miss Green knew what she was doing, I reassured myself. Undoubtedly, there would be a beneficial purpose to this very odd *tree of feelings,* which now took pride of place on its own slightly more colourful wall at the centre of the classroom.

After school, Mr Flatley stood in the middle of the stage on a podium, set up in the gymnasium by the very grumpy caretaker, Jimmy. The dance master was as excited as a young boy waiting for the latest Xbox to arrive at Christmas. He was absolutely enthralled to see so many children had arrived in attendance for his first after-school Irish dancing club of the year, clapping gleefully as we all entered.

I was feeling nervous but determined to be more confident, or at least act it anyway (notice how I am already becoming more able to identify my feelings... maybe Miss Green *was* on to something).

Jenny, Martha, Edna and even Sienna had signed up. I was glad to hear it was the first experience for all of us, except for Martha. Edna informed me she was a bit of a professional, having represented Mayo in an All-Ireland Irish dancing competition a couple of years ago.

Surprisingly, some of the boys, Billy and the Adamson twins, had also signed on the dotted line.

It suddenly dawned on me what I was signing up for. The thought of trying to make my body look like it could have rhythm in any way made the contents of my stomach start to gurgle.

Enthusiastic as always, Jenny was quickly changing into a pair of dancing pumps that looked much too narrow for her feet.

After noticing what Jenny was doing, Mr Flatley's Irish dancing assistant, Amy Arnold, quickly made her way over to her.

"No need for pumps today," she said. "We are just explaining the rules and going through a couple of basic starter steps today."

Jenny let out a loud sigh.

Sensing her deflated mood, Amy decided to let her off with wearing them. Instantly, my friend was back to her cheery self.

"Thanks, Miss Arnold," she grinned. "I knew you weren't as strict as those other ones say you are."

Amy walked on, dumbfounded at jovial Jenny's remark.

About twenty minutes passed, and Mr Flatley had talked us through a really dull PowerPoint presentation about the rules and regulations of being in the dancing group. Then after a laborious talk from Jimmy, the grumpiest caretaker of all time, about how to best care for the wooden gymnasium floor while dancing, we stood in separate spots going through some 'basic reel' steps.

Strategically , I had made my way to the very back of the hall, so there would be no one behind me watching me clumsily attempt to move my legs with some form of grace. Edna had decided to join me at the back; I think she was feeling every bit as confident as I was. She couldn't help giggling every time she tried to move. It was nice to see her look happy, not as bored as she usually did.

I could see Amy Arnold was horrified (but clearly trying to hide it) at the sight of me attempting to take part in my fur-lined flipflops.

"Maybe you could take them off and try to dance in your socks," said Amy.

Bella had made me special socks that fit nicely into flipflops to keep me extra warm, as the sea wind in Alcora was gradually becoming crisper by the day.

"I can't really dance yet," I replied.

"Well, yet is the key word here. You *are* going to be a dancer," she smiled.

I wished I had felt her confidence in that.

Reluctantly, I took off my furry flipflops and set them in the corner behind me.

Mr Flatley stood again at the front on his very own, man-made stage, separate and made for his feet only, he informed us all.

Thankfully, at a very slow pace, he showed us the 'jump 2,3s' next. We had to try to keep in time with him before we had to practise on our own. Fortunately, Billy Barlow pleaded with him to show us the steps again one more time (for about the ninth time) before we started off on our own.

My heart skipped about five beats as I saw Mr Flatley a few minutes later, during our solo practice, clip-clapping speedily down the huge hall towards me, legs flinging above his head, as per usual.

"Felicity, isn't it?" he asked as he arrived beside me, not ceasing to keep those invincible pins of his out of the air for a second.

"Yes," I replied, pointing my right toe to the floor as he had instructed and trying the confusing routine for him - very unsuccessfully.

Edna still chuckled loudly beside me. I was trying my best not to burst into a fit of nervous hysteria.

"That's good," he observed. "Shoulders back, back nice and straight... Make sure you hop high... like this," he demonstrated, swinging his arms at my feet. I tried to look like I understood.

After about three painful minutes of personal coaching, it was Edna's turn. He began to fling his way over beside her. *Phew!!!*

At the end, Mr Flatley showed us a video clip of him dancing in a show in New York about ten years ago. He was on stage surrounded by a team of astonishing, mesmerising dancers performing completely in time with each other. He seemed to have been one of the main parts in the show. It was purely dazzling. The flamboyant, foot-flinging Mr Flatley really was a gifted Irish dancer.

When the session had finished, I felt so relieved to have made it through my first ever Irish dancing lesson and was pleasantly surprised at how much I had enjoyed it. Miss Green was right about it being therapeutic – the only things I had focused on were my feet and unfit legs for that short time, and I felt good. Good is 'not a feeling,' according to Miss Green - *I felt fulfilled.* The fact that all of us, apart from Martha, had started off as clueless as each other had maybe made it a little bit easier.

Jenny, although finding some of the steps extremely tough on her breathing, had managed to do some of the 'jumps' quite well. She almost left a hole in the floor and had been growled at by *Jolly Jimmy,* as I'd started to call him, but she didn't let this put her off. I felt so proud of her. I decided to tell her how well she had done as we walked towards the late bus home.

"You were great, Jenny," I commented as we climbed the steps of the school vehicle. "You took to it really quickly, and you never gave up."

"Thanks," she smiled back at me. "I didn't think I'd make it through those last jumps... my legs were like jelly," she chuckled. "Like two wobbly jellies, slipping and sliding in ice cream."

I was astounded at how she always laughed at herself and wondered what she really thought - or if making a joke about herself was a sort of disguise. I was starting to truly like Jenny Jackson and admire her.

"Are you going to go to Sienna's birthday party?" she asked me as we took a seat beside each other on the bus.

"When's that?"

"It's on at the weekend," she replied. "She was running around asking everyone to go there, after the class. She said for me to make sure I asked you, too."

Suddenly, I felt sorry for Sienna again. Surely the numbers were low.

"I might go, actually. What are you thinking? Yes, or no?" I asked.

"I think we should all go for a laugh and get a good look at Miss Fancy Pants' house and all those acres of land," chuckled Jenny. "Ponies, hens, monkeys... goodness knows what else she has!"

"She has monkeys?" I asked.

"I don't know; I wouldn't be one bit surprised," she answered.

"Me neither," I replied. "We'll have to come up with a plan to convince the others to go."

During registration the next morning, Miss Green was determined to make good use of the *tree of feelings.*

After calling out our names individually, we had to choose an *honest* leaf from the tree about how we were currently feeling as we 'started off with our day' and share it with the class. My neck went blotchy red, and both palms began to sweat as she reached Edna Evans. That meant *Felicity Flanagan* was coming up next.

"How are you feeling today, Felicity?" she asked a few seconds later, looking at me with encouraging eyes.

"Relieved!!" I instantly blurted out.

I couldn't believe I had managed to speak. One word it was, but...

I. Had. Spoken. Out. In. Class.

Now, I was genuinely feeling relieved! The best type of relieved you could ever imagine. And proud. And delighted. And happy. And successful.

Miss Green was overjoyed.

"Wonderful!" I am feeling very proud of you, Felicity," she remarked loudly. I thought she was going to get up and do a victory dance.

After a short pause, she added, "Next time, I'd like you all to try to explain why you think you are feeling a certain way. Identifying a feeling will do for today, though," she beamed.

Yes.

Agreed.

Enough.

For.

Today.

When Sienna Sorski's turn arrived, I had never seen as wide a smile on her face and such eagerness to talk from her. EVER.

"I am feeling VERY excited!" she exclaimed, bouncing in her seat.

"Great," replied Miss Green.

"Can I tell you why now? Explain?" asked Sienna eagerly.

"Yes, you can," answered the teacher, surprised.

"It's my birthday at the weekend and... and..." she stuttered, "lots of the girls are going to come to my birthday party!"

She was clearly overcome with happiness (for a change).

"I'll not be going," Edna mumbled to me under her breath.

I had a bit of work to do on her, I reconfirmed to myself.

"That's very kind of you, girls," said Miss Green, scanning the room and acknowledging all females, like we were *all* going to be in attendance at the birthday bash. The rest of the girls in the class, apart from our little group, had never spoken much to Sienna. Only when forced to during paired or group work. And even then, it was the bare minimum of conversation.

Billy Barlow's hand shot up.

"Yes, Billy, would you like to ask something?"

"What about some of the boys? Can we not go?" he asked, looking across at Sienna with pleading eyes.

"Emmm," hesitated Sienna, "maybe... I mean... if you want to?"

"Yes!!" yelled Billy. "I'll be there! I'll be there to get a look at that ranch of yours!"

Sienna was a bit unsure of how to react to that. I could sense she was confused at why people were actually willing to go to her party. It didn't really matter that they didn't like her though, the fact was, her classmates were going to attend a party of hers for the first time in her history of going to school.

The school week went by really quickly, and Miss Green had successfully managed to encourage us all to talk about our feelings. Even me. Every member of the 6A class was able to identify a feeling (from the tree or one of our own choice) and explain or kind of describe why we thought we might be feeling that way.

She genuinely believed this was purposeful, and I suppose it did make us more aware that people are good at hiding their real feelings and pretending things were okay, even when they were far from it. It did kind of encourage us to reflect on our emotions and be honest. Or try to be. It felt liberating to share them. Most of the time, that is. Of course, sometimes, we weren't always sure why we were feeling a particular way. Our feelings could be a case of waking up in a mood or getting out of bed on the wrong side, as our teacher often called it. Sometimes, we would choose not to share and that was okay, too.

I was certainly proud, happy and relieved that I was speaking out a bit more. It was a major breakthrough for me, in fact. I always went a bright, beaming shade of red, a bit like a ripe tomato (from the bottom of my neck to the tip of my forehead), but I was managing one or two word answers. Things were looking up.

Dawn M. Gelston

CHAPTER 7

BIRTHDAY BASH AND BERTHA BRAWLS

Saturday, the day of the birthday party of the century arrived, and I had surprised myself by having managed to convince Edna to go. This was after a considerable amount of begging and a reminder from me that there would be no expense spared, the prediction that we would *probably* get party bags filled with extravagant, luxurious gifts and the best variety of food served by waiters, a firework display and maybe our own horse to ride back home on (perhaps this was a slight exaggeration on my part, but it had worked).

Martha Molloy had agreed to go out of curiosity, and, Jenny... well, from the start, she was eager to see the mansion Sienna lived in, too. The idea of food in abundance had contributed to her instant acceptance of the party invitation.

Sienna's driver, Frederick, an extremely tall French man, arrived at the door at 12 pm on the dot. He pointed towards an extra-long, red limousine out the front with the 'Sorski Diamond Jewellery' logo painted across it.

"The rest are all patiently waiting for you, mademoiselle," he smiled.

Bella dashed from the sewing room covered in thread and measuring tape to bid me farewell and make sure all was safe, as she always did.

"I will pick Felicity up at 6 pm," she informed Fred.

"Zat is no problem, pas de problème," he replied, with a strange look, like he was almost offended that I would be collected from the party.

Jenny's head popped through the sunroof as I excitedly made my way to the luxurious car. My first ever limo ride.

"Yo, Fel!" she cried, with a mouth full of food. "This thing is CLASS! You're gonna love it!"

I quickly hopped into the back. The others were chatting loudly and munching on enormous bags of popcorn and swigging from cartons of juice: Martha, Edna, Billy and one of the twins, Adam (I had learnt Adam had a dimple on his chin and Alan didn't).

The twin-less twin had his feet stretched out beside him on the long, sofa-like seats and was throwing popcorn into the air and trying to catch it in his mouth. Edna looked the least impressed out of them all.

"This better be a good day," she remarked as her eyes met mine. I hoped for my sake it *was* going to be one to remember.

Billy was pointing a remote control he'd helped himself to, and a huge, widescreen TV slowly started to appear at the front of the lush, extra-lengthy limo.

"Look at this!" he said, like he'd just created the invention himself. He was captivated.

"Look," said Martha, passing me a piece of paper, "we have an itinerary for the day."

The fancy, pink, glittered piece of paper read:
Sienna's 11th Birthday Party Itinerary:
12.30 pm: Milkshake Reception (Drawing Room)
1 pm: Outdoor Activities of Choice - footgolf or pony riding
2 pm: Farm Walk
3 pm: Indoors - Party Food (Dining Room)
4 pm: Dancing (Dance Studio)
5 pm: Choice of Activities-swimming in pool, mocktails, go-karting
6 pm approx: Home Time
**Events/schedules are subject to change, depending on punctuality, group choice, etc.

"Starting off with milkshakes and drawing," I commented.

Martha cackled loudly, "Not drawing! In the drawing room!"

I looked at her blankly.

"A drawing room is a posh name for a big, fancy living room."

"Oh," I replied, feeling my neck quickly begin to turn into a tomato again. "Never heard of it," I admitted.

"Yeah, only really rich, posh people would have them," she added. "There'd be one of them, or at least one of them in, say...Buckingham Palace ."

"Ahh..." I nodded.

"No mention of party bags," interrupted Edna, "or our own horses."

"No, but I'm sure we'll have a laugh," I said, grinning back at her.

"A day we'll never forget, I'm sure," she replied, unenthused.

A few minutes later, we were ushered through huge, cast-iron, electric gates by a sleepy-looking, extremely broad-shouldered security guard.

"What would they need security for?" Jenny gasped.

"Well, they do own a diamond jewellery company," Billy replied.

"Oh, yeah," answered Jenny, nodding slowly, like it suddenly made sense.

"I'd say there's millions of euros worth of diamonds in this place," added Billy.

"I doubt they'd want to keep them in the house!" hissed Edna, rolling her eyes.

I hoped she was going to snap out of the foul mood she was in soon.

As we drove in through the gates towards the house, the sight was like something from a period drama (the ones Bella loved). There was a perfectly-mowed garden, the size of a football pitch and, at the far end, stood the most lavish, beautiful, two-storied house I had ever seen in real life. You could probably have fitted twelve of Bella's house inside it. At least.

As we drove up the long, tarmac driveway, the limo echoing with *ooooohhhhss* and *wowwwwssss* from us all, I spotted Sienna standing on the steps of the house waving erratically.

We all jumped out of the limo before the very offended Frederick could reach the door and stood for a few seconds, taking in the sight of the majestic mansion before us. Sienna sprinted down the steps and stood awkwardly in front of us.

"Welcome!" she beamed.

"Happy Birthday!" I said, reluctantly handing her the small gift bag containing a book voucher and knitted scarf, courtesy of Bella.

Now that I had witnessed the extent of her wealth, I was really embarrassed at my meagre present.

"Thank you!" she grinned, "I'll open this later."

I was so relieved. AGAIN.

Everyone else, apart from Martha, wished her a happy birthday, as we entered the grand house behind the rich, posh birthday girl.

Inside, we again stopped in our tracks and stood gawking at the marble-floored hallway and golden, spiral staircase that led to what looked like about twenty other rooms.

Excitedly, Sienna ushered us to follow her towards the drawing room.

She stopped at the door before opening it.

"Choose whatever you like in here, but we have party food later on too, so probably better not to go too crazy just yet," she advised us, directing her eyes towards Jenny the most, I noticed.

She opened the door, and Billy Barlow charged in before the rest of us.

It was a monstrous, marvellous room. The biggest living room I'd ever seen. It had two wooden treat carts set up inside, both attended by smiling servers. One of them was an ice cream station, with about thirty different flavours to choose from. The second cart was a chocolate and sweets station filled with copious choices: Freddos, Chomps, Curly Wurlys, Mars Bars, Minstrels, Maltesers, Skittles, strawberry laces and marshmallows, to name a few.

"Choose which ice cream you'd like first. They'll make them into a thick milkshake, and then you choose your fillings for them," said Sienna, pointing towards the stations of sugary dreams, "they'll be the thickest, creamiest milkshakes you've ever tasted."

"Can we mix and match the ice cream?" asked an eager Jenny.

"Yes, of course, you can!" replied Sienna, looking at her like she'd asked her the most ridiculous question ever.

We all moved towards the ice cream station in a fast-moving cluster, and were greeted by its happy-looking waiter.

"Martha, I know you like mint chocolate chip, so we ordered three different types," said Sienna, smiling at her.

"Thanks," Martha mumbled without looking at her. She fixed her eyes on the sensational spread of ice cream.

About fifteen minutes later, we all sat happily on large throne-type seats, scoffing out of huge pots of chunky, creamy milkshake. Sienna was right; they were the thickest I'd ever tasted, and the creamiest, and the best. She'd forgotten to tell us they'd be the nicest thing our taste buds would ever enjoy. Delicious was an understatement. Jenny and Martha were at the sweet carts going for seconds. Billy was licking the inside of his carton like a cat enjoying the last of its milk.

Unexpectedly, the door swung open, and a very cheerful, flexible woman lunged into the room.

"Hello, my lovelies," she smiled, showing off a set of sparkling teeth. I think the woman had the most teeth I'd seen in a human being's mouth.

Sienna sighed quietly and rolled her eyes up towards the glistening chandeliers.

"I am Lydia, and you are all very welcome to Miss Sienna's birthday party."

"Oh..." said Martha, from the sweet station, "you're the maid."

"Maid?" asked the horrified woman. "I'm Sienna's nanny!"

"What's the plan now?" interrupted Sienna.

"The ponies are set up in the field; shall we go?"

After a bit of a heated discussion, pony riding had won over footgolf and was going to be the first activity of the day.

Several minutes later, we were all kitted out in jodhpurs, helmets and riding boots, ready to embark on our pony ride. I had hesitantly taken my flipflops off, but Lydia had promised to keep them in a special safety box for me while we were out on the ponies. She really had thought of everything.

Waiting on the party-attendees in the field, were our own, individual ponies and one-to-one riding instructors. I had never ridden on a pony before, but with help from my personal instructor, Tamara, I swung my legs up and was able to hop on straight away. I was chuffed with myself. I was also extremely glad the riding expert was going to be standing beside me the whole time.

Jenny struggled a little to get up initially, but with the help of two of the instructors, she managed to swing her legs onto her brown and white pony. Billy needed a bit of support to climb on from his instructor, a bemused-looking man from Belgium.

A short while later, we were all confidently cantering around the field. Adam had ridden before, so he took the lead at the front beside the birthday girl. Even Edna was enjoying it.

Sienna was the happiest I had ever seen her. She looked back at her classmates like we were the best thing she'd come across in her life, even for a very wealthy and privileged young girl.

We had made it about three times around the field when, out of nowhere, Jenny's pony began bolting off away from the rest of us at fast speed. Her instructor was still grabbing on to the reins, sprinting and battling to hold on and keep up with them. The small horse suddenly came to a halt, and the instructor swung around mid-air, landing on her back.

Jenny was yelling at the top of her lungs.

"Get me off, get me off!!" she cried, "I'm going to be si…"

And before she got her words out, Jenny had flung her head over the side of the pony where her instructor was laying shellshocked, and projectile vomited all over the poor woman. The vomit flew from her mouth like water shooting out from a garden hose. The disgusted, distraught instructor was covered in white, lumpy vomit from head to toe.

"So sorry!!" screamed Jenny, awkwardly climbing off the pony as fast as she could and kneeling down beside her to try to help.

It was one of the funniest moments of my life. Of all our lives. We all guffawed loudly. My jaw was hurting from laughter.

Shocked and horrified, the woman eventually managed to get up on her feet and she began to attempt to wipe the smelly contents of Jenny's stomach from her face with her sleeve. She was retching loudly, fighting the urge to vomit herself. Sienna rushed over on Precious to help them.

Back at the changing room a short while later, we were still laughing at Jenny's antics. Edna had found it the funniest and was winding the vomit-fiend up about it.

"I mean Jenny, why didn't you just be sick over the other side of the pony?" she asked her.

"I... it happened too quickly," she answered, still really embarrassed. "I hadn't time to think... it just flew out of me!"

"Next time," mocked Martha, "please consider where you're going to spew first. Please be sure to avoid other people!"

Again, we all erupted into high-pitched fits of roaring laughter.

Sienna arrived in the middle of the cackling chorus to remind us that the farm trip was next on the agenda, and Billy started to dance a 'heel, toe' Irish jig with excitement.

"I LOVE, LOVE animals!" he said, breathless from all his jigging around. "They make me want to break into dance... Irish dance," he giggled, amused at himself.

"What type of animals do you have?" asked Adam, seeming excited too.

"We don't have typical farm animals," answered Sienna. "That's all I'm saying."

As we walked towards the farm, a noisy green tractor pulled up beside us. A blonde-haired, slightly weathered-looking man grinned at us from the driver's seat.

"Hello there, folks!" he smiled. He had a top tooth missing at the front and a kind, friendly face. "Pleased to meet you all, so I am," he continued.

"This is Finbar," Sienna informed us. "He looks after the animals for us."

"Ahhh... you're their personal farmer then?" asked Billy.

"I am a farmer, but I wouldn't quite say that, so I wouldn't," he answered.

"I've my own farm over yonder, so I do!"

He pointed to fields behind him. "Don't need to be a personal farmer to anyone, so I don't. I make me own way in this world, so I do!"

"Cool," answered Billy, seeming a little teary-eyed with embarrassment. I hoped he wasn't going to start to cry. He'd been doing so well recently.

"You can hop into the trailer there, so you can," said Farmer Finbar, pointing to the back of the tractor and a wooden box with four wheels.

"We can't all get into that!" protested Martha.

"Why not? It'll have you at the farm in no time – safe as houses, so it is," the farmer smiled encouragingly, again proudly showing off the large tooth gap at the front of his mouth.

Lydia backed him up. "It'll be fun; jump in!" She ushered us towards the trailer.

Seeing her chance to cut out some walking, Jenny was the first into the back. She lifted her leg onto one of the trailer wheels and pushed herself up in less than five seconds flat. Maybe she was getting fitter, I thought.

Less than a minute later, the tractor let out a loud groan, and we were off down the dusty lane, all plonked on our bottoms on the cold floor of the trailer box.

It felt like we were actually going on some sort of exciting adventure, yet to be revealed.

Lydia stood up at the front, chatting to Finbar as we went. I looked around at my fellow classmates, and realising that I had very quickly made many new, interesting friends, I began to feel very grateful (stolen from our tree of feelings, of course).

Billy and Adam were sniggering at being transported in the back of a farm vehicle, travelling at high speeds of 15 miles per hour.

"Yeee haaa!" yelled a happy-again Billy, as the wheels of the trailer jumped out from a pothole on the laneway.

"Hold on to your hats, folks!" shouted Finbar. "It's a bumpy one, so it is!"

"I'll need to go to the hospital after this," scowled Martha. "Who knows what animals were last on the back of this thing, too!"

Everyone ignored her.

Sienna looked embarrassed.

"This is great fun," I reassured her.

She smiled back, appreciating my remark.

We pulled up outside a large, metal shed with no windows. No way of guessing what was awaiting us inside, I sighed. The stench of manure caught the back of my throat and, the others' too obviously, as we all sat pinching our noses.

Sienna hopped out of the trailer and sprinted towards a long, metal pole with a button at the bottom. When she pressed it, the pole sprouted out arms that started swooshing out scents of sweet aromas, like lavender mixed with roses, into the air. I was awestruck by the invention.

"I know; the smell is disgusting," said Sienna. "But this will help us while we're here."

"You've your own outside air-freshener machine?" gasped Martha.

"I don't know which smell is worse," said Adam.

I nudged him.

Lydia, as nimble as always, jumped from the back of the box and helped us by taking each of us by the arm when it was our turn to jump off.

"You are in for a real birthday treat," she said, smiling at Sienna.

"What's in the shed?" asked Edna.

"We'll not go in there yet," Lydia answered. "We will walk towards the field behind the shed, first."

We all followed the adults.

Finbar, who was now walking alongside Lydia, was much taller than I'd imagined, about 6-feet tall, at least. He was covered in brown, dried-in muck from the tips of his wellies to the top of his boiler suit. Unsurprisingly, this didn't seem to bother him. Or Lydia, for that matter, who was looking up at him, entranced as she walked. She was literally about half the height of the friendly farmer.

As we were nearing closer to the field, Finbar ran off ahead of Lydia. Lydia requested that Sienna close her eyes for a surprise.

The nanny brought us all to a standstill, and Sienna stood awkwardly, holding her hands over her eyelids. She was hopping from foot to foot with excitement.

"Don't say a word," ordered Lydia, as Finbar came towards us.

He was holding a lead at each side of him.

Edna was squealing with laughter, and I had to whisper to her not to let the secret out.

"Wow," said Billy.

"What is it? What is it?" Sienna repeated.

'You can look now,' said Lydia, even more thrilled than the rest of us.

Standing right in front of us were two very graceful alpacas, one brown and one white, dressed in bow ties and top hats.

Sienna screeched with happiness as soon as she opened her eyes.

"You got me alpacas!!" she yelled.

"Well, they're not actually yours, so they're not," said Finbar.

"They're on loan for a little while," added Lydia nervously.

"Ohhhh," replied Sienna, looking disappointed.

As if suddenly realising she was coming across as very spoilt in front of her audience, she added some gratitude.

"Thanks so much! Thank you!" she smiled at her nanny for the first time.

"Look at the one on the left, standing with its nose in the air," chuckled Edna.

"The one on the right has the funniest teeth," said Billy, walking towards it, holding his arm out to pet it.

"Let the birthday girl go first," said Finbar, directing Billy to stand back. "We'd better approach them in groups of two if we can, so we would... we don't want to annoy them too much, so we don't. Although they do love people, so they do."

"Ever seen alpacas before?" Lydia asked the group.

"No!" we all yelled in chorus.

"Not in real life anyway or ones dressed in their birthday bests," tittered Edna.

About fifteen minutes later, after we all had posed for photographs and selfies beside the hairy, hilarious-looking, South-American mammals, we were on the way back toward the shed we'd first avoided to see pot-bellied pigs, apparently. After about twenty bouts of begging from Billy, Sienna had agreed she would tell us every other farm animal we were going to see.

Sienna had seemed bored of the alpacas very quickly, and Lydia's face couldn't hide her disappointment at the birthday girl's short-lived enthusiasm; she really was *very* spoilt.

We were marched quite quickly toward the shed by Sienna, who couldn't contain her amusement at introducing us to the pigs. I wasn't so sure how these muck-loving, oinking animals were going to be received by the group. Martha, surprise, surprise, was not one bit impressed.

"Pigs are really, really smelly," she mumbled as we approached the doorway.

"There are air fresheners in the shed too, don't worry," said Lydia, over-hearing her.

We were led in by Sienna, who directed us towards a large pen on the left. There were patches of manure all over the crusty, concrete floor, and it was like winding ourselves through an obstacle course to avoid them as we made our way across the outhouse.

"Needs cleaned up in here," said Sienna, directing her words towards Finbar, who seemed to be pretending he didn't hear her.

"They are let out of the pen for a bit of playtime, from time to time," said Lydia. "They can't be cooped up all day; they enjoy a run out in the field, too."

"Meet Bertha," said Sienna, pointing to a fat, black pig lying with her legs in the air, on top of a mound of muck and manure.

"Bertha doesn't look like she does much running," laughed Billy.

"She could do with a good run around, right enough... she's like me," giggled Jenny.

"I don't think that tummy of yours could do any running today, Jenny," jested Martha.

Bertha *was* possibly the broadest pig ever known to man. Her face looked like it had been blown up by a bicycle pump, and she was the proud owner of about four chubby, wobbly chins.

"I love her," said Sienna to the group. "Look how happy she looks."

Edna replied, "As happy as a pig in sugar."

"Haven't heard that one before," said Finbar. "I do know another one, mind you, so I do."

"Best not share that one," interrupted Lydia.

"It's not, so it's not...you're right there, so you are," he replied.

"Wouldn't it be great to be like Bertha?" asked Lydia, staring at her with admiration.

Eventually, noticing there was a litter of about ten other pot-bellied pigs grunting and roaming around the same pen, Adam asked, "Do the rest of them have names?"

"They look so much smaller," said Edna.

"We have a Charles, a Diana, a William, a Kate... you get the gist," said Lydia.

"A royal family of pot-bellied pigs," chuckled Adam.

"No Camilla, mind you," added Lydia. "We don't like her as much."

"Bertha isn't a royal, is she?" asked Martha.

"No, I think emmm....Bertha just looked like a Bertha, we thought, so we did when we got her," replied Finbar.

"Is she not called after your aunt?" asked Lydia.

"Emm, no, no...she's not, so she's not," replied an embarrassed Finbar.

"My mistake," said the nanny.

"That's meant to be a secret, so it is," he whispered to her.

After about five minutes of pleading, we eventually convinced Finbar and Lydia to let the pigs out for a bit of playtime with us, into the centre, concreted part of the shed. Only Martha objected a bit.

"I don't want them running around my feet," she whined.

"Ah Martha, they need a bit of freedom," Adam told her.

Bertha was up on all four feet in a flash when she heard the gates of the pen open. She moved with far more speed than we had imagined. Or wanted.

As she ventured through the gate ahead of the other, much-smaller pigs, she looked around at her human companions, and the speed of her walk became progressively faster.

All of a sudden, her short legs quickened, her head bowed, and she started to run towards us like a charging bull. We scattered in different directions, shouting and running for cover. If she made contact with you, you'd be on the ground as flat as a pancake in one split second.

Only two others aside from Bertha had decided to make it out of their imprisonment.

"Bertha, where has all this energy come from?" yelled Sienna.

Finbar stood with his arms out in a very brave attempt to catch her, but she galloped straight through his legs, toppling him right over onto a patch of sticky, stinky manure on the cold, dirty ground.

"Bertha, you're a brat, so you are!" he wailed, gathering himself up onto his feet and rubbing an expanding bump on the side of his head (another slab of muck on his boiler suit wouldn't annoy him).

"You're like a woman possessed, so you are!" he added, his face purple with anger. I wasn't sure if she understood English or human chat, for that matter.

Bertha was headed towards me next, and I sprinted towards the doorway to try to make a swift exit. As I picked up some speed, one of my flipflops fell off - the right one. Within a split second, Bertha had reached it, scooped it up into her chunky mouth and had turned in her tracks, dashing as fast as she could, belly wiggling, bum wobbling, chins flapping, back into the pen.

"Get her!" I yelled. "She has my flipflop!"

My heart had jumped into my throat. *What was I going to do?*

Seeing my distress, every one of my friends tried to run after beastly Bertha but they were slipping and sliding through the clumps of manure, now smeared right across the floor of the shed and all over their party clothes. Unfortunately, they were all too late. Much too late.

Lydia had quickly tried to close the gate to stop her from getting back into the pen, but the gate caught on the ground and wouldn't budge.

The dangerous, devious, pot-bellied pig galloped back into the pen, plonked the flipflop on top of her manure mound and was now lying on top of it, pushing it deeper into the pile of muck with her broad, pudgy back.

It was like she was teasing me. She was evil. I couldn't believe it. My hands were dripping with sweat, and all I could think of was trying to cope without it. What was going to happen?

Tears began to travel down my cheeks, and I stood in the middle of the shed, my bare right foot now covered in pig secretion. I was so humiliated that I was crying because a pig had stolen my shoe. My flipflop.

"We'll get it, we'll get it!" said Lydia, hurrying over to console me.

Edna was at my side, patting me on the back.

"It'll all be fine in the end," she reassured me. "We will get it back."

"What if she eats it?" I asked in despair.

"She won't eat it," said Sienna, who'd made her way to stand beside me without me noticing.

"You didn't tell us Bertha was a shoe-stealing, shoe-burier!" yelped Martha.

"It's not Sienna's fault," I said, sensing how bad she would be feeling about it.

Finbar had told us all to stay at the doorway of the shed and demanded Lydia help him from inside the pigpen.

"I don't know what's happened to her," said Sienna, who was still practically standing open-mouthed, nodding in disbelief at the actions of her pet, pot-bellied, petulant pig.

"Adam! We need you up here, too!" yelled Finbar.

The very excited young man had made the journey to the outside of the pen within two seconds. Pointing towards shelves in the corner, Finbar ordered Adam to put on a pair of gloves and some wellies first, and when the overjoyed ten-year-old leapt into the pigs, he handed him a spade almost twice the height of him. The farmer stood preparing him, for what seemed like three hours, for what he was going to do to help them recover the flipflop.

Adam was engrossed and nodded proudly back at Finbar, acting like he'd just been chosen to represent his country in the Olympics.

"How come he's asked him and not me?" asked a perplexed Billy, whose skin was practically turning a shade of olive green with envy, right in front of us.

"Maybe as he's taller," answered Jenny.

"Yes, that's it, I'm sure," added Martha sarcastically.

"We can help, too!" shouted Billy.

"All good for now, so it is!" shouted Finbar. "You all stay right back!"

All eyes looked towards me. I knew they were all concerned about me, but nothing seemed to help how I was feeling.

"I'll never be able to wear them again," I said hopelessly.

"How will you not?" asked Sienna.

"Would you wear shoes reeking of pig dirt?" I snapped.

"Em... no..."

"Sorry," I replied, now feeling pangs of guilt as well as hopelessness jumping around in my chest. "I know it really isn't your fault."

"We'll get you new ones," Sienna replied.

"I've had them for years, Sienna; I can't. I *won't* wear new ones."

Our conversation was interrupted by the loud commotion going on inside the fenced pigpen. Lydia and Finbar were holding a large piece of material like a bedsheet at opposite ends. Adam stood a couple of metres back, ready to swing into his role, and Bertha was lying cheekily with her legs in the air again, grunting at them. I never thought I could hate a pig more. I wanted to cook her up in a frying pan and eat her for dinner. And I don't even eat meat.

The two adults lay the sheet onto the ground beside Bertha, and Finbar quickly, with a very strong push and shove, rolled the fat lump of a pig off the mound and on top of it. She spun from the pile of manure, shrieking an ear-piercing squeal as she went. It sounded like a fire alarm going off, right inside your ear drum. Her legs tried to fight what was happening, but she was too fat to roll quick enough off her back and escape.

Finbar and Lydia both held opposite sides of the plastic sheet the pig now lay on and scooped it into the air. They were, with great difficulty, holding her as high above the ground as they could. Adam automatically sprang into action, digging frantically through the manure mound with his spade to find the flipflop.

The rest of us stood at the doorway, transfixed at the sight before us. As Lydia was so much smaller than Finbar, the sheet was like a lop-sided hammock, and, at one time, it looked like the pudgy pig was going to fall off. I secretly hoped they would drop her from a huge height.

Both adults had beads of perspiration dripping from their foreheads. They closed the pig inside the sheet and walked the five-tonne weight as fast as their tired legs could carry them to the opposite side of the pen, as far as was possible from the mound of pig faeces. Abruptly, they set the sheet containing the shoe thief down on the ground. The fat pig winced and struggled to stand. Finbar stood in front of her this time, with his legs pushed together, blocking her path.

"You're not getting past this time, so you're not!" he shouted at her.

"Have you got it?" shrieked Lydia. A yell that said, *please tell me you have!!*

Adam was currently running from the mound with a spade. When he had made it outside the pen, with his gloved hands, he scrambled through the shovel and pulled out the manure-laden flipflop.

Holding it in the air like a gold medal he had just actually won at the real Olympics, he yelled, "It's here! I've got it!"

There stood the triumphant young boy, his arm and face sprayed in putrid pig manure, with my fluffy flipflop, barely recognisable. It was in one piece and covered in Nutella-coloured pig droppings, but Billy had managed to get it back. I wasn't sure how I would get rid of the stench. EVER. But the relief I had felt was like nothing I had experienced before. My friends, I could tell, also felt an enormous sense of ease. I looked over at Billy, and he was patting his eyes with the sleeve of his t-shirt.

'Happy tears, these are happy tears, for once!" he smiled at me.

I really did have the best friends in Ireland; I reminded myself.

"I wonder if the air fresheners would help?" asked Billy as we returned back to the house.

"Doubt that very much!" said Martha, walking through the hallway.

We all still, apart from Martha, looked around the mansion entrance in amazement. I'm not sure you would ever find this type of splendour normal.

Our farm trip had been cut short, too, but no one seemed to mind. Today wasn't the day we'd get to see mountain goats or naked-neck chickens. That would have to wait.

Back at the house, we went straight to the shower. There were over ten bathrooms, so there was no waiting around. I couldn't wait to get my feet and body rid of the thick manure and revolting smells.

We were each given tracksuits to wear home, ones with 'Sienna's Birthday Party' and a picture of ponies printed on the back of them. The velour outfits were also made to fit us all perfectly, of course. The boys' were black, and the girls' were purple.

We gathered in the dining room for the party food. I didn't feel like eating but was trying my best to tuck into the savoury spread of vegetarian and non-vegetarian sausage rolls, sandwiches, pizza, chips, burgers and sausages that had been laid out by a catering company, who'd been hired specially for the day.

"You are welcome," Adam had answered when I thanked him for the fifteenth time for saving my treasured flipflop. "I was tempted to hit big Bertha with the shovel," he giggled.

Finbar arrived a little later and was all freshened up, wearing a blue shirt and jeans. His hair was sticky with gel; he looked very clean. Really clean. Lydia appreciated his effort the most.

"You are looking fantastic," she grinned from ear-to-ear at him as he sat down at the table opposite her.

"Thanks," he answered shyly.

"The slipper... I mean flipflop, has been hosed down, Miss Felicity, so it has," he informed me, "and is currently in a bowl of water and Vanish, so it is."

"A bowl of water and what?" I asked him, confused.

"You know: that nice, smelly liquid that shifts any smells or stains... Vanish!! I use it with me overalls, so I do, and it removes all sorts of muck, so it does."

"Thank you," I replied, trying to look enthused.

"An hour or two in there, a dry with the hairdryer, and that shoe will be like new, so it will," he added.

Billy, who was happily sitting at the head of the table, held up a sausage.

"Here's to our Bertha!" he cackled.

Sienna didn't find it as amusing as the rest of us.

"I don't know what happened to her; she's never behaved like that before!" she shouted out, still clearly baffled at bolshy Bertha's behaviour.

"Only thing I can think of... she's had a change of medication, so she has. Maybe that's it; she has had trouble with her bowels, you see," said an also-confused Finbar.

"Maybe not the best time for that discussion," interjected Lydia, reaching across the table and patting him on the arm.

"Maybe not! Sorry! I'm sorry, so I am!" he replied, laughing lightly, "my brain runs off with me, sometimes, so it does."

After we had finished eating, the biggest birthday cake I'd ever set eyes on or was likely ever again to set eyes on arrived at the table. It was a pony cake - a mini replica of Precious. It took Finbar and Billy both to carry it and set it down in front of Sienna.

Jenny had secretly told Lydia about how Billy had been upset at not being chosen to help retrieve the flipflop, so the kind-hearted nanny had asked a blissful Billy to help with the task.

I looked at Sienna as she blew out her candles, surrounded by friends and her nanny but an absence of parents and, at that moment, I realised we were more similar than I'd ever thought before. Her eyes looked a little sad, and I *again* felt conflicting sympathy for her. I knew how it felt not to have your mum and dad around on special occasions. This was for different reasons, but still as difficult for her. I was sure of that.

When the cake had been passed around, and a sizeable chunk of it devoured, we were escorted to a dance studio at the back of the house. There was a dancing DJ, flashing strobe lights and everything an 11-year-old would ever wish for at a disco: glowsticks, disco balls, glow-in-the-dark face paints, as many drinks as we wished and mini-trampolines. I wondered what might go wrong next, and hoped for the birthday girl's sake, that the rest of the day would go okay. Even just semi-okay. P-L-E-A-S-E.

We all partied until we were dripping with sweat. We had a dance-off competition, won by a very happy Martha. No one cared and no one mocked the other person, even when Jenny thought dancing like a chicken laying an egg was a 'cool' dance move.

Lydia and Finbar joined us for a little while, but Sienna was embarrassed at the flexibility of Lydia's dance moves and her, yet again, deflated nanny took the hint and left after a few minutes. I was rather impressed that she could do the splits so easily.

"She only wanted to have some fun," I told Sienna as I noticed Lydia leaving, with another look of disappointment and sadness etched across her little face.

"I know," replied Sienna.

"She cares about you, too," I said.

"I know…I guess she's the closest thing I have at the minute to a mum, so… no one wants to see their mum dance and backflip in front of their friends, right?"

"I suppose you're right," I answered with a smile.

"I am so sorry about the flipflop, Felicity," added Sienna.

"It's okay."

"It's not okay."

"It is," I answered. "Once Bella gets her hands on it and re-lines it with new material or whatever, it'll be like new again."

"She can do that for you?" she asked, surprised.

"Yes, she can do anything with her hands really," I replied. "She's an awesome dressmaker."

"Sounds like she's really cool."

"She definitely is," I grinned back at her. "Now let's have a go on the trampolines," I said, pulling her by the arm to the other side of her very own dance studio.

Later in the afternoon, the boys had decided to venture to the go-karting track, and the girls had eventually come to an agreement that a splash in the heated, outdoor pool was going to be the final activity before home. We decided we needed to cool down after busting so many moves on the dance floor.

After our swim, we sat cheerfully, lazing on sun loungers (ironic in Irish autumn, I know) beside the enormous, 40 metre by 40 metre swimming pool, sipping from sugary mocktails served by our own waiter.

Lydia had given us fluffy dressing gowns, and our personal pool attendant had placed heated lamps above our seats to help keep us warm.

I took the opportunity to encourage some Sienna appreciation from the others.

"Thanks for the great day, Sienna," I said. "Apart from… well… Bertha, I've really enjoyed it," I smiled.

Jenny gulped down the last of her fourth 'strawberry delight' mocktail before adding, "Me too. Thank you, I've loved it, too," she nodded. "I hope the riding instructor is okay, though."

"She'll be fine," Sienna replied.

"You wish you could say it happens all the time," giggled Martha, actually showing slight warmth towards the birthday girl, for a change.

'Yeah, but unfortunately, I can't," Sienna laughed. "Did you both have a good day?" she asked, looking at Edna and then back to Martha.

'I did,' said Edna. "Plenty of laughs. I could get used to living like you do," she added, looking around at all the grandeur as she spoke.

"And you, Martha?" she repeated.

"I did too, thanks. I umm... I liked the ice cream."

"Great," Sienna replied, glad she'd asked Lydia to source a few different mint chocolate variations for her.

At that moment, Lydia came prancing towards us, holding an iPhone. She swiftly handed it to Sienna.

"Your mum is on FaceTime and wants to wish you a happy birthday," she smiled at her.

Seeming really embarrassed, Sienna was up and had quickly walked to the other side of the pool in less than about ten seconds.

"You liked the ice cream?" Edna asked Martha. "That's all you liked from today... that's all you could say?"

"Well, I *did* like the ice cream."

"Nothing else?" Jenny inquired.

"You don't feel in any way bad for her? What does Miss Green call it... empathy? Any empathy for her?" Jenny asked her.

"Why should I?" shouted an enraged Martha.

The rest of us protested together by tutting and sighing loudly.

"She might look like she has the best of everything, Martha," I added, "but she really doesn't. Her parents aren't here on her birthday."

"Well, I'm glad you can speak out now!" she answered me.

"Oi!" snapped Edna. "No need to be cheeky to Felicity!"

I was gobsmacked.

Sienna arrived back beside us, and we all sat in awkward silence for a few minutes before Lydia came back at the pool to tell us all it was almost 6 pm: home time.

Bella was astounded when I told her about the antics of the day on the way home in the car. The flipflop was placed in the boot, in a box filled with potpourri, in a bid to get rid of the last scent of pig smells.

"I will make you some new, scented lining for both of them, don't worry," Bella, as expected, had reassured me. "I have to finish off the-banshee-bride's wedding dress this evening," she giggled, trying to lighten the mood. "But I'll try to get them sorted for school on Monday."

TRY? WHAT DO YOU MEAN ONLY TRY? I wanted to yell at her. The thought of not wearing them for the day filled me with dread and fear. I had never gone one single day without them, not since the day my Gran had bought me them on holiday in Spain, about five years ago.

I was a little worried that people would know one of them had been covered in a small mountain of animal faeces and then rolled on by a gruesome, grotesque pot-bellied pig. But, I was already impressed at how Finbar's strategy of dunking the flipflop for a couple of hours in water with scented stuff and blasting it with the heat from a hairdryer had shifted a good bit of the pong.

I thought about Finbar and what a kind man he was, and I laughed to myself, remembering how Lydia had acted around him. He was a nice man, and I was disappointed not to see him to thank him again before leaving for home. Lydia told us one of his cows was in labour, so he'd driven up the laneway at full speed in his green, rowdy tractor to help save the day. Yet again.

I wondered what it would be like, living a life like his, helping others and looking after animals all day long. Today's scene with Bertha was maybe slightly out of the norm for him, but he handled it very well and acted quickly... a little like me with the priest, I suppose. He certainly seemed more of a fight-reactor when faced with dilemma... also, a bit like me. I wanted to be more of a fight-reactor all the time, though, I thought, as I remembered my silence in response to being spoken to like that by Martha earlier.

One day, I hoped I'd be able to stick up for myself properly.

I had thanked Lydia several times before Bella arrived for me and I received a tight, awkward hug from the thoughtful nanny before heading out the door. I had the feeling she didn't get the chance to hug Sienna like that.

I slept that night as soon as my head hit the pillow. The day's events had left me exhausted and drained, but I could nod off, satisfied that my flipflop was saved, currently on my bedroom floor, still in a bed of scented, dried flowers. I drifted off, content that Bella would work her magic on it.

On Monday morning, I was grateful to be putting my newly-lined, flower-scented flipflops on with my school uniform. I actually didn't really care what anyone thought now, so long as I could still wear them. Not even comments from that terrible trio, first thing in the corridor, made me feel any less proud to be wearing them.

"Ugghh, I smell pig crap!" said the triplet boss as I walked towards the 6A classroom.

"Ugghh, I smell pig crap!" repeated the other two in sync (unsurprisingly).

With my nose in the air, I walked straight past them and into the classroom, not letting on I'd even caught one glimpse of any of their nasty, curly-mopped heads.

Miss Green announced there would be no mass this morning but instead a short assembly of 'celebration' in the gymnasium. It didn't bother me or any of us, really. It was still time out of lessons, and we were all glad we didn't have to walk outside in the bitter, Mayo morning air.

As we entered the hall, Mrs Rodgers was doing her usual tornado spin of the room, demanding children hold their sore index finger against tightly-pursed lips.

Bowman looked even angrier than usual and was chastising a young child for talking. She was shouting at the top of her lungs, hunched over him, spraying the poor youngster with that dreaded, disgusting, salty saliva and pointing the walking stick in his face.

She nearly jumped out of her skin when she turned around to see Father Brennan standing behind her. Her jaw literally dropped, and it was brushing along Jolly Jimmy's beloved gymnasium floor when she realised that he had just witnessed her venomous rant.

"Father Brennan, you... you are here early this morning!" she stammered, picking her ugly, pointed jaw up from the ground.

I chuckled to myself. I glanced over at Miss Green, who today adorned pig earrings (of all things), and could see she was even more thrilled than I was that the hideous headteacher had been seen as her true self by the school priest.

"Ms Bowman," gasped Father Brennan. "I am beyond horrified to have witnessed how you have just spoken to someone else's child... one of God's children!"

She tried to make her measly excuses.

"He wouldn't do what he...."

"I do not care what he would or would not do," he interrupted. "And to think, you are leading the way for children's mental health and wellbeing across County Mayo," he continued.

"*SHE* is leading the way for what?" squawked Miss Green across the hall. "Now that is a laugh and a half! Apologies, Father Brennan, but that really is ludicrous!"

He either ignored what Miss Green had said or didn't actually hear her right. He was still fixated on Ms Bowman.

"You should be ashamed of yourself! I hope this isn't normal practice!" he continued, directing his words towards our hateful headmistress.

It was now Bowman's turn to stand there like a scorned child, her head bowed in shame.

The priest turned his back to her and marched up to the front of the hall, too disgusted to stay and look at her frightening face.

"And as for that walking stick," he raised his voice, "stop using it to scare school children! We're not living in the 1900s!"

Bowman still stood there, in the same position for a couple of seconds. I didn't know whether to feel sorry for her or not. No, no, no, I assured myself, that woman didn't deserve the slightest drop of pity or any of the new word we'd recently learnt about... *empathy.*

Several minutes later, the scorned headmistress was falsely smiling beside Father Brennan on the stage. The still-disgusted priest snatched the microphone from her, continuing to hold a dismayed look at her on his face. A gold trophy was perched on a small table in front of where he stood.

"Children of St. Bernadette's, as I'm sure you are all aware, a week ago, while celebrating mass, I very unexpectedly and very unfortunately began to choke..."

Edna nudged me and used her head to point at the table.

"That's yours," she whispered.

Surely not, I thought. Please...no!!

I didn't hear any more of his words. I stood there, dazed. Edna nudged me with her elbow, wakening me from the blur.

"Felicity, they're calling you up. Go!" she said. "Go Felicity, go! You deserve this!"

I felt like I was having an out-of-body experience. Through the cheers and clapping of the whole school, I eventually made it up the steps to the stage. I mustered all my energy and strength to walk to the middle, to stand beside the priest. The crimson neck blotches were back, and the sweat had well and truly broken on my hands. I looked into the crowd and caught sight of the jealous heads of the Turner triplets, standing with twisted, envious mouths, all exactly the same. A strange switch flicked on inside me, and I went from feeling overwhelmed with nerves and embarrassment to feeling the proudest I had EVER felt.

I smiled down at the crowd and spotted Miss Green, who was waving and cheering the most out of everyone. It was hard to miss her.

For her, I thought, I am going to try to enjoy this moment as much as I possibly can.

"Anything you would like to say?" asked the priest, after thanking me sincerely and handing me the trophy: the first-ever St. Bernadette's Bravery Award.

I took a deep breath and prayed the trophy wouldn't slip through my sweaty hands.

"Emmm... Emmm..." I stuttered. "I'd just like to say you are welcome, Father Brennan, and I'm emmmm... I'm glad I was able to help you. Thank you."

"No, no Phoebe... or... I mean, Felicity. It is me who owes you thanks."

I couldn't believe I was able to speak. I could hardly manage to spit out more than two words in class and, there I was, standing in front of the entire school, being able to (quite articulately) speak a full couple of sentences. Not exciting sentences, but still, I'd said them. *What had just happened?*

The longer I stood there, the less nervous I had felt, and I was even happy to have my photograph taken. Father Brennan informed the whole audience this particular image would be framed and placed in the school entrance hallway for all to see.

"The first-ever winner of The St. Bernadette's Bravery Award," he smiled, "not sure there'll ever be a winner more worthy of this award."

Obviously, the photograph taking pride of place in the school reception was news to Bowman's ears, as her slimy tongue and wrinkly, protruding jaw had hit off the ground yet again as he announced it. I wondered if she was starting to feel tired of picking her manky mouth off the floor. She was bound to be - it wasn't the first time I'd witnessed her do it today alone. I giggled to myself.

Dawn M. Gelston

CHAPTER 8

JOYFUL JOLLY JINGLES

In the next few months, a few things happened at St. Bernadette's Primary School. Unfortunately, Bowman was still in charge; we're not that lucky.

Here's a short summary of the latest developments:

- We *all* regularly attend the Contemporary Celts after-school club, and I am VERY surprised to have become reasonably good at Irish dancing. Biggest shock ever!
  Mr Flatley is my biggest supporter, constantly telling me how he 'sees something unique in me'.
  It's been therapeutic for me. I take my flipflops off to wear my dancing pumps, which were handmade by Bella, of course. I have still been wearing them every day. Not every hour of the day, though.
- Sienna is eventually becoming more accepted in our group, even though it is, at times, with some disdain from Martha. Our spoilt friend is also trying to be less snappy with Lydia, and they have been becoming closer by the week. She now talks about her nanny with slight admiration and a lack of eye rolls.
- Jovial Jenny has been trying her best to lose weight. Abstaining from eating so many bags of her favourite Tayto Cheese and Onion crisps is helping her, and the Irish dancing classes are keeping her fit. She has also joined a walking club at lunchtime. Miss Green is, of course, very pleased with this and praises her efforts continuously. She has made it clear to anyone within earshot that Jenny is losing weight for health reasons only;

she is beautiful as she is and should never change.

- Bowman and her bog breath have been trying to redeem themselves in Father Brennan's eyes, and she actually admitted to him that Miss Green was the one taking the lead in mindfulness and mental health and wellbeing across the school and county. The humpy headteacher is now all for this (or so it appears) popping into classes during the sessions and joining us to do mindfulness activities on occasion. She even managed to stay for a full session one afternoon and had nodded off, lying on one of the smooth, cotton bean bags (good old Enya again had contributed to the headteacher losing consciousness too, no doubt).

- Miss Green has been attending mental health conferences and has been lobbying for health and wellbeing lessons to be part of the school curriculum in the UK and Ireland-she may even be going to go to England to appear on ITV's This Morning with Phil and Holly!

- The tree of feelings has made its way around the school. Each classroom has its own version being used daily in a great attempt to help children cope with and understand their changing emotions.

- Mr Flatley is still clip-clapping his way around the school. Although, not long ago, he slipped one morning on a recently-mopped floor and hurt his coccyx quite badly. Dance classes are still going ahead, though and he can still manage to fling his feet five metres above ground (of course).

- Father Brennan kept to his word, and my happy face is still hanging for all to see in the entrance hall of the school. I actually do feel proud about this, and I am happy to admit that my confidence is very gradually improving.

- Bella is eventually getting recognition for her phenomenal wedding dress creations. She has been chosen to showcase a selection at a Wedding Wonders fashion show (a very famous Irish wedding magazine) in the new year. She is delighted about this and is busy working her magic with material. Donna's dress made it to the altar, by the way, without causing any damage to her internal organs. As a gift, she has given Bella a weekend stay at a five-star hotel in Dublin. We are taking a post-Christmas trip.

- Mrs Platt's custard is still curdling and churning in peoples' stomachs, but the more experience I have had at forcing it down my throat with a swig of water or diluted juice, the easier it is becoming. I have been pleased to find out that ice cream is on offer on alternate weeks. It's nothing like the ice cream we'd had at Sienna's, but less rancid than the custard. Jenny has still been helping me out when she can, by discreetly finishing the contents of my bowl, but I think Religious Rodgers is on to us. She always seems to linger around our table during the Tuesday Treat days.

- Jolly Jimmy has still been obsessing over his gym floor. Bella told me he had been doing that when she went to St. Bernadette's well over twenty years ago, so this was never ever going to change. Well, until he retires. Eventually.

As it was now December and the lead up to Christmas and the holidays, we had been rehearsing for the end of term assembly. Apparently, these assemblies are usually based around a nativity play theme, but Miss Green had decided 6A's assembly was going to be one called "Different" - a celebration of differences in people.

Unlike other years as well, we had to practise individually or in pairs, and our performances were not going to be revealed until the day of the assembly. Even our classmates didn't know what we were going to do. Well, only the other children we were paired with. This meant Miss Green was working tirelessly with us after school for weeks now. She was so dedicated and kept saying how she thought the messages in this assembly would be some of the most powerful ones yet.

The morning of the assembly had arrived, and as I was leaving for the bus, Bella called out to tell me she was really looking forward to seeing me up on 'that stage.' My tummy flipped a little at the thought of going on to *that stage* and being the centre of attention, but I was very prepared and ready, I reminded myself.

As I was coming off the bus, Sienna quickly ran across the playground to meet me.

"You'll never guess what's happened!" she said breathlessly. Before I could answer, she continued, "Lydia and Finbar got engaged!"

"That's great!!" I replied enthusiastically. By the look on Sienna's face, I wasn't sure if this was good news for her or not.

"This means she'll leave me too, though."

"Oh..." I managed to reply.

"She says she won't, though, and they won't be getting married for ages yet."

"She loves you, Sienna; she won't leave you."

"I don't know; everyone does... everyone leaves..."

"Well, if she does, you can come and live with me and Bella."

"Sure where would Precious go?" she instantly asked. "You don't have a field... I couldn't leave her," said my pitiful friend.

89

"You won't have to worry about that," I reassured her as we climbed the crooked, concrete steps into school, walking past my large, framed, cheesy grin and trophy-in-hand photo in the hallway.

As soon as we entered the classroom, Martha and I were hurried out and ordered to make our way into the changing rooms at the back of the gymnasium to get ready. Our teacher meant business today and wasn't wasting a second.

Martha and I were performing as a pair and were opening the performance. I was glad as this meant we could get it out of the way and hopefully enjoy the rest of the show. I had no idea what the others in the 6A class were going to do. It was exciting.

As I zipped up my Irish dancing costume, I was startled to hear a voice shouting my and Martha's names.

"Martha, Felicity, come out to the stage... we need to have our pep talk."

Martha rolled her eyes.

"Just to put our pumps on, and then we'll be out, Mr Flatley," she called.

"Quick, quick!" he yelled.

Moments later, the three of us were on the stage, group hugging like a world-famous band about to perform at Wembley stadium.

"You've got this, girls... don't be nervous; you dance like two magnificent swans... the best I've seen at this school in a very long time. Do yourselves and me proud today!"

"We will!" we replied together.

I was less nervous, having Martha with me. Although she was more experienced than me, I felt almost on par with her. Rehearsing every night after school and even on the weekends had helped me feel more secure in my ability to dance. I loved Irish dancing, the music, everything about it. It made me feel free. I could forget about everything and only focus on what my feet were doing.

Mr Flatley introduced us on to the stage as being two of the brightest Irish dancing stars he had come across.

"Our dance today is a dance with a twist... and something a little different from the norm," he grinned, "fitting in nicely with the theme for today."

Bella was about two rows from the front and clapping almost as fast as the speed of light. She was literally going to burst with pride.

Miss Green and I had practised breathing techniques to help when I felt nervous, and I started to put them into action to control my trembling body. I noticed Martha subtly dry her hands on her dress when she let go. My hands had been so sweaty (as always).

When the music to 'Dance Monkey' kicked off, the whole room cheered. Much more than I'd ever expected. Just as we began to dance, my right foot slipped, and I stumbled on the floor. It was definitely more slippery than usual.

I T-H-O-U-G-H-T I W-A-S G-O-I-N-G T-O E-X-P-L-O-D-E!

The music stopped suddenly, and all I could hear was a stinging, buzzing sound in my ears and loud gasps from the audience. I did not want to meet Mr Flatley's eyes. I was so afraid I'd really disappointed him.

Noticing, Martha took me by the hand and pulled us back a couple of steps from the front to start the routine again.

She whispered, "I've got you; we've got this!"

With a nod from Martha to the music teacher, the music started again. I took a deep breath, and I am not sure how I managed to refocus, but I continued to dance my Irish dance routine mixed with a touch of hip-hop. I danced like my life depended on it, with the most enthusiasm I could muster.

Five minutes later, I stood again holding Martha's hand and bowed in front of the audience. The crowd stood up on their feet. We had a standing ovation! I had never felt more thrilled. Not in my whole eleven years and eight months of existence. I searched the crowd to find Miss Green, and I gave her the widest grin. She had tears in her eyes.

We quickly changed out of our dance costumes and made our way to our allocated seats to watch the rest of the entertainment from our class. Our class teacher was now on stage, chatting to the audience about the importance of children knowing the power of being 'different,' embracing their identities and not being forced by anyone to change what they like, feel or believe in.

Although some looked slightly unsure, most of the parents were nodding in agreement with Miss Green. When she had finished speaking, she received the warmest applause, especially from her 6A pupils. Best. Teacher. In. God's. Kingdom.

Jenny was next up. She made her way onto the stage, and her group of fans all screamed in support of her. She had a bright pink dress on and her usual pigtails, one yellow and one blue ribbon hanging down at each side of her ears. She looked so pretty.

"I have a poem I would like to share with you to tell you all what it's like to be a person like me."

"Our Jenny!! Go, Jenny!!!" Edna yelled!

Rodgers looked like she was actually going to collapse with a heart attack at Edna's outburst and, in a matter of seconds, made her way to silently and subtly scold her. Edna did not care in the slightest and shrugged her shoulders back at the angry teacher.

Jenny smiled, "I will begin," she said, clearing her throat. "My short poem is called *Proud To Be Me.*"

She paused for a moment and then began to recite very slowly.

"One day... someone is gonna love me,
For who I am, not just what they see,
I'm more than just what I look like... I'm me,
I've strength, great friends, an amazing fam-ily,
How would you feel if it was your sister, your brother, your cousin they teased?
Not fun then, is it? You see?
I embrace being different from the norm; I'm loving it, not the McDonald's type
(she giggled), I'm just happy with being me,
Why shouldn't I be?
I'll never conform to soci-et-y... what they think I should look like or what I should
be,
So as you sit and judge others for being different... just think...
You need to believe... you need to see,
We are all people; we can be ourselves and choose our own identity!"

After a few seconds, she said, "Something for you all to think about."

The elated Jenny then finished with a confident curtsy in front of the grateful audience. The entire upper school St. Bernadette's cohort, led by the Year Six children, all stood up and began banging their seats on the gymnasium floor in support of our amazing, unique and inspirational Jenny.

As quick as a lightning flash, Jimmy sprinted to the stage and grabbed the microphone, rather curtly, from Jenny's clasp.

"No banging on that good floor! I will put you out for that," he roared, "and ban you all for life! You selfish..."

Miss Green immediately took the microphone from him before he could finish with a tirade of abuse.

"I absolutely agree with Mr Johnston," she said. "Well, maybe not about the banning for life part," she added, muttering under her breath. "Please show your enthusiasm only by clapping, or we will have to remove you from the gymnasium."

Parents sat with their mouths ajar at the children's antics. Either that or the threats from the school caretaker. Both probably. Blobs of sweat started to appear on Bowman's forehead. Jimmy began to look a bit faint, and the PE teacher passed him a bottle of water which he necked in one ginormous gulp.

"What a wonderful, thought-provoking poem from Jenny," continued the teacher. She had chosen eagle earrings to fit in with today's assembly theme, she had informed us earlier.

"All her own words too," she smiled, applauding the performance again.

The crowd clapped along with our teacher, using only their hands this time; it seemed like they had taken the warning seriously.

Jolly Jimmy was clearly relieved to see this, and his heart rate seemed to decrease as he left the stage.

Next to the stage was Billy Barlow. He stood in the middle with great confidence, a wide smile spread across his face.

'Well done to Jenny," he said. "Fantastic poem."

He continued to stand centre stage with the charisma of an experienced game show host. Our next performer slowly walked to the side of the stage and lifted a guitar off one of the seats.

I couldn't believe my eyes. No one could. When did Billy learn to play guitar? I really wondered how he had managed to keep this a secret from us all. From his crew.

Edna suddenly appeared on the stage beside Billy, and he started to strum on the guitar. He. Was. Incredible.

The two of them burst into a rap, taking alternate lines.

"So what if I'm a boy and I cry?" (Billy)

"Don't make you any less of a guy!" (Edna)

"You see the trouble with the world these days..." (Billy)

"Hiding emotions, hiding feelings, people afraid..." (Edna)

"To choose their own clothes, own style, live their own lives..." (Billy)

"We're all human, we all go through tough times..." (Edna)

"Let's make a difference to the world..." (Billy)

"Both guys and gals..." (Edna)

"Look out for your friends, your pals..." (Billy)

"Let them know it's okay to talk when stuff gets heavy..." (Edna)

"It's okay to shed a tear, to cry..." (Billy)

"People are too good at covering things up, making a disguise..." (Edna)

"It's about time we all realised..." (Billy)

"We only get one life..." (Edna)

"Live happy, do as you want, no strife..." (Billy)

"Express your feelings, your emotions..." (Edna)

"Whether a girl or guy with pride..." (Billy)

"Don't be ashamed, don't hide..." (Edna)

"Set the way for this and the next generation..." (Billy)

"Take the lead..." (Edna)

"We all need to listen, take heed..." (Billy)

"Live lives where our mental wellbeing is just the same as our physical needs..." (Edna)

"About time this was realised... this was agreed... Be happy, choose your own path... be---lieve..." (Billy).

He raised his guitar in the air in a dramatic finish.

The two classmates walked to the front of the stage, held hands and took a well-timed bow. The room erupted. Even Bog Breath looked impressed.

The duo went off the stage, overwhelmed with the reaction of the crowd. I was going to burst with happiness.

For about forty minutes, uninterested, we sat through the rest of the performances from others in our class: a magic show, a unicycle performance and lots of singing, to name a few.

Sienna came on last and was pulling nervously at her dark, shiny hair as she began to speak.

"Today is about being different... so I have decided to open my farm at the weekends for ch... il... children," she stammered, "for... for free!"

"Go, Sienna! That's our girl there, so it is!" yelled a familiar voice from the middle of the hall. "You go, girl!!"

I looked round to see Finbar standing up and fist punching the air. Lydia wagged her hands above her head from the seat beside him.

The adults' antics were enough to tip Religious Rodgers right over the edge. She looked like she was at her limit and could drop any second.

Sienna's nervous frown changed to a glistening grin.

"Those of you who know me," she said, "will know this is definitely me being different; me being open to change."

"How kind of you!" said Miss Green on the microphone as she made her way up to the front again. "What a wonderful, thoughtful thing to do, Sienna! Simply amazing!"

Our teacher, along with Sienna, then summarised what this would look like, hours of opening and showed the leaflet Sienna had made to advertise her extremely kind gesture.

About two minutes later, a triumphant Sienna had enjoyed her warm applause and had left the stage. Bony Bowman had made her way up to close the show. She stood slightly but not as badly hunchbacked as normal. Maybe this was her way of trying to be different.

Adam Adamson suddenly appeared on the stage and said there was a surprise that no one knew about. After a minute or two of fidgeting around with the interactive board at the back of the stage and a mobile phone, he informed the crowd he was ready to begin. He had frozen a video on the screen and then pressed play on the remote control.

"Watch closely," he said.

The footage, taken on a mobile phone, had very limited, mumbled sound, and initially, it was hard to make out what was happening in the recording.

You could not hear as much as one breath in the whole gymnasium as we all watched the Turner triplets on the video. They were crazily spraying and smearing cans of Pledge furniture polish right across the stage. It took a few seconds to register, but it then became clear that they were setting a slippery trap for the performers in the assembly! The boss one was chuckling as she went about her menacing mission, her two sheep following her orders to use their feet to splodge the substance around.

"This was at 8.55 am this morning!' Adam commentated loudly. "Not long before Martha and Felicity were due to dance! That explains why Felicity's foot slipped at the beginning, doesn't it?" he asked the crowd in disgust.

We were all witnesses to their scheming and scamming antics. Hundreds of us. They. Were. Caught. Red-handed.

The silence quickly turned to more gasps, tutting and disbelieving muffles. Then those hundreds of heads started to scan the room, trying to pick out the horrible, spineless girls.

Adam interrupted, telling everyone to keep looking.

"There's more!" he announced.

Bowman suddenly appeared beside him. "That's enough, young Adamson," she said. "Mobile phones are not allowed at school!"

Mr Flatley interrupted her, "Let him continue!" he demanded.

Bowman scurried off stage, her face deep purple with rage.

All heads in the audience tuned in, eagerly awaiting the next revelation.

"This was a few minutes afterwards!" Adam continued.

The video showed the two 'sheep' sneakily entering the gymnasium with a mop and bucket. They seemed to be attempting to remove the liquid trap that was set to cause me and my partner, or both of us, to fall. I could not believe my eyes. No one could.

"How did I miss this?" roared a yet-again distraught Jimmy.

An ear-piercing wail made its way from the back of the hall.

"How could you do that? How could you do that to me? Your sister?" It was the wickedest one.

"We couldn't let you do it!" answered one of them, the other triplet copying two seconds later.

"We couldn't let you do it!"

Bog Breath was now marching the metre sticks down the centre of the hall towards them, her hunched body moving, unaided by the walking stick, the quickest it's ever moved.

"We're different! We're not like you!" yelled the recently-brave one.

How fitting, I thought.

Bowman eventually reached the trio before they could continue shouting. In a louder-than-usual, croaky voice, she ordered them out. Immediately.

The girls promptly scarpered from the gym hall. Not together for once. The boss one, rapidly losing her title, followed her sisters a few steps behind, her head bowed, and tail caught right between her legs.

Meanwhile, on the microphone, Miss Green desperately tried to attract the crowd's attention back up to the front, but was failing miserably.

Clip-clap-clip-clop sounds started all of a sudden from centre stage. It didn't take long to draw the attention away from the girls. The new gasps floating around the gym were those of amazement again. Thankfully, Mr Flatley's flinging, fierce legs were doing the trick.

Miss Green suddenly flung off her high heels and began to Irish dance alongside the Deputy Headteacher, who looked as baffled as the rest of us by her actions. At once, he competed against her, catapulting his legs as high and as fast as he could. She was almost able to match him and his speed. She was astounding.

Mr Flatley practically elbowed her out of the way to get the most attention mid-stage. It was hilarious to watch him openly envious of our teacher's dancing skills.

Around ten minutes later, after both teachers tired out, the crowd again stood to applaud them. Mr Flatley looked so proud of himself, perhaps happy he had slightly outdone Miss Green's efforts. Through waves of whispers, the audience slowly made their way out of the gym. The triplet incident was sure to be the talk of Alcora town for a very long time.

Back in the classroom, after commending our teacher's choreography skills, we were stretched out in our favourite spots, chatting about the girls' actions.

Miss Green was being as optimistic as always.

'We'll certainly have learnt something today, won't we, children?"

'Yesss..." echoed twenty-seven weary voices.

"Everyone at that assembly has," continued the class teacher. "Your messages were strong. Impactful."

"Those were the messages you taught us," I answered her. "You've taught us to be strong."

"Thank you, Felicity," she smiled a little awkwardly, fixing one of the eagles in her ears.

"Yes, Miss. *You* make a difference to all of us," added Billy Barlow.

'That's very kind, children," she replied, her eyes welling up. "That's what I'm *always* here for."

"Okay to get it out again, Miss?" Billy asked her, pointing towards the guitar.

'Great idea!' she answered. "I'll put the words up."

Without hesitation, every wacky, wonderful member of our gang, along with the rest of the 6A class, rose instantly and formed a semi-circle. With our teary-eyed, extraordinary teacher, we rapped along together, shouting out loudest when we came to the words...

"Let's make a difference to the world..."

We were happy. We were content. We were loved.

AUTHOR BIO

Dawn M. Gelston is a primary school teacher and qualified journalist currently living in Dubai. Throughout her teaching career, she has taught hundreds of children in Ireland, Scotland, England and now the United Arab Emirates. Dawn has experience working with children from various backgrounds. She is passionate about teaching emotional health and wellbeing, describing it as paramount in educating children growing up today. Dawn pays tribute to the children she teaches, who she describes as the most unique, inspiring and supportive young adults she has been privileged to meet and educate.

Felicity Flipflops is Dawn's debut novel and is a story of how empathy, encouragement and friendship can positively impact children's lives. Underpinned with humour and a touch of emotional wellbeing, the book will appeal to children aged between 8 and 12 years old and can be enjoyed by all the family.

Use this page to record what you have learnt from reading the book.

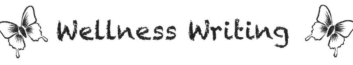

Wellness Writing

★ Sharing my feelings with others is

★

★

★

★

★

★

★

★

Use this page to record what you have learnt from reading the book.

 Wellness Writing

 Sharing my feelings with others is

Printed in Great Britain
by Amazon

78879857R00059